OXFORD JADE

CYNTHIA E. HURST

Milestone Agency

Victorian Mysteries 5

ISBN: 9798397391863

Author's Note:

The city of Oxford needs no introduction, except to note that this book is a work of fiction and the characters and situations portrayed here do not represent any actual persons, businesses or academic institutions. Some locations are also partly or completely fictionalized, including Holy Trinity Church. St Clement's Church, however, is quite real, and renovations to it in the 1870s were largely funded by the wealthy Morrell brewing family.
Oxford Prison was located on the site of a Saxon castle largely destroyed during the English civil war. It was also extended and modernized in the 1870s, with men, women and children all imprisoned there. It served as a prison until 1996, and is now a heritage and tourist attraction, which includes the appropriately named Malmaison hotel.

Details of the Preston case can be found in 'Oxford Blue', the first Milestone Agency Victorian mystery. Jem first appeared in 'Oxford Ivory', the third Milestone mystery.

This book uses American spelling.

ONE

Had it really been only a year?

Rose Miles stood in the doorway of Holy Trinity church and stared into the dim interior of the building. The pews, the altar, the lectern – everything was exactly the same as it had been during her last visit. That had been little more than a year earlier, but it seemed a lifetime ago. Not only that, but she felt as though she was a completely different person now than the one she had been then.

A year ago, the last time she had set foot in the church, she had been swathed in black mourning clothes, numb with shock and trying hard to keep from looking at the coffin holding the body of her husband Edward. She'd barely registered a word of the funeral service and had responded to well-meaning condolences without really knowing what she was saying.

Rose had not been back to Holy Trinity since then, and had rarely attended church at all. One reason was that she didn't want people who knew her to point and whisper. Sympathy in those early days was hard enough to bear, but now she would be identified as the young widow who didn't know how to behave properly.

Another reason for staying away was that her faith had been severely shaken by Edward's untimely death. It was no good people assuring her that it was God's will and

3

everything happened for a reason. Rose simply hadn't believed that, feeling blame should be laid more at the hands of the drunken driver whose carriage had collided with the one in which Edward was riding. And what was the divine reasoning behind leaving her a widow at twenty-five?

She had felt in those early months more as if she'd been thrown into a prison cell, forced to dress in unrelieved black and forbidden to venture outside her home. Friends had stopped calling and she had been discouraged from doing anything that suggested she was not mourning properly. She missed Edward and the life they'd had together, but once the initial wave of grief had subsided, she'd been frustrated, resentful and bored to tears.

So one sunny spring day when she could bear it no longer, she had thrown caution and decorum to the winds and taken a short walk. That scandalous action had turned her life upside down.

"Are you sure you want us to be married here? We could have the banns read at St Clements, you know, where my parents attend services, and have the wedding there. I'm sure I'm still considered a member of that church even though I haven't been for a while."

Rose turned to look at the man by her side. Theodore Stone was the reason her life had altered beyond recognition, to the extent that now, a year after she had been widowed, she was engaged to be married again. Theo, she knew, understood her reaction to Holy Trinity and her memory of Edward's funeral, but was tactful enough not to mention it.

"St Clements is rather a good church, spacious and quite modern," he was saying, "My parents even manage to ignore the fact that another brewing dynasty rather than ours paid for the recent renovations. But it's your decision, Rose."

Rose had only been to St Clements once, but she remembered a long central aisle paved with decorative tiles, a small forest of pillars and far too many pews.

"I think St Clements is rather too large, don't you? It's not that I want to hide away, but neither do I want us to rattle around in an empty space, since we are only planning a small, quiet wedding."

"Indeed. It was just that you seemed a bit apprehensive."

Rose took a deep breath. "Not exactly apprehensive, but hoping to lay past memories to rest. We both live in the Holy Trinity parish, after all, so the banns would need to be read here, even if we were to be married elsewhere. And it's the church we are most likely to be attending in future. So I think it's the best choice."

"A very sensible decision, and one I am happy to concur in. Shall we hunt up the vicar?"

The vicarage was next to the church, and as they walked up the flagstone path to the door, Rose rehearsed what she might say if her decision to marry again was queried. It was not inconceivable that a widow might remarry after a discreet interval, but a year was not considered discreet. It wasn't even decent, as far as most people – including Rose's mother – were concerned.

She had compounded this disgraceful behavior by accepting the marriage proposal of someone who could be considered unsuitable. A man who, however good-looking, well-spoken and charming, came from a family engaged in trade, a word spoken in invisible quote marks by upper class families such as hers. And not even a respectable form of trade, as far as they were concerned, but a brewery, for heaven's sake.

Rose had not intended to fall in love with Theo, or indeed with anyone; it had simply happened over the past few months, to the extent that she could now not imagine life without him.

Theo lifted the brass door knocker and Rose braced herself.

After a long pause, the door opened and a woman in a gray dress who was plainly the vicar's housekeeper looked at them curiously.

"Good morning," Theo said. "Is the vicar available that we might have a word with him, please?"

"He's out visiting parishioners," the housekeeper said, sounding annoyed that Theo wouldn't know this.

"Oh, I see. It's just that my fiancée and I are hoping to marry here and wanted to ask him to have the banns read."

The housekeeper's gaze went from Theo to Rose, who smiled politely. She couldn't remember seeing the woman before and hoped the lack of recognition was mutual. Maybe they should have gone to St Clements, after all, where Theo might well be recognized but she wouldn't be.

"Vicar'll be back about eleven," she said. "I'll tell him you've been. Your name, sir?"

"Stone. Theodore Stone."

"I'll let him know."

"Thank you. Would it be all right if we just had a look inside the church?"

The housekeeper frowned, as if to indicate that anyone contemplating getting married in Holy Trinity should already be familiar with its interior.

Rose said hastily, "I live nearby, but I'm afraid I haven't been to a service here for some time. And Mr Stone has never seen the church."

"I see." She frowned again, perhaps at the sight of Rose's black coat, bonnet and gloves, the last vestiges of mourning. "The charwoman's there, I think, but yes, you can have a look."

"Thank you so much; you've been very helpful," Theo said, giving her a warm smile.

They went back around to the front of the church and Rose said, "You can be quite charming, Theo, can't you? If I had been on my own, she would have turned me away, I'm sure."

"I do my best." Theo grinned and held the wooden door open. "After you, my dear."

The scent of old damp stone and candle wax greeted them as they stepped inside. Rose looked around, confirming her first impression that nothing had changed in the past year. That included the cold interior, and she remembered having to wear a heavy cloak or coat to keep from shivering when attending services with Edward.

"It's not bad at all," Theo said approvingly. "A trifle chilly, but we can dress warmly, and after all, the marriage ceremony itself shouldn't take very long. Then we can repair to somewhere warmer for the wedding breakfast."

"I don't want a fuss made, Theo, you know that. Just our families and a few friends. I thought about perhaps just inviting them to the house afterwards."

"That sounds ideal."

Rose felt a little guilty, because after all, Theo had never been married before, even if she had. She might have felt better if she had realized Theo was so thrilled she had agreed to marry him that he wouldn't have objected to any venue – or indeed any other detail of the wedding – she might choose.

Like her, he was under no illusions that their marriage was going to be warmly received by everyone, although his family had been more willing to accept Rose than her family was to accept him. That only made him more determined to prove he would be a worthy husband for her.

They were recalled from their separate thoughts by the rattle of a mop against a tin pail and the appearance of a plump, middle-aged woman with an apron over her dress and a mob cap covering her hair. She lugged the pail into the central aisle and wrung the mop out before plopping it onto the stone floor.

Theo and Rose watched as if mesmerized as she pushed the mop back and forth, leaving a swathe of wet floor in its path.

"That's a thankless job," Theo said softly. "I suppose it needs to be done, though, to keep the dust down."

The charwoman was ignoring them, and Rose imagined she was used to people dropping in while she worked, since a church was meant to stay open for those who wanted to pray or meditate outside of the scheduled services.

She pictured herself and Theo standing at the front of the church while the vicar read the wedding service. She would wear something demure, suitable for a second wedding, and Theo, who always dressed smartly, would wear his best suit. Her sister Helen and one of Theo's three brothers would be their attendants; their collective parents would be in the front pew, and …

"Glory be," said the charwoman, setting her pail of water down with a thump. "It's the toff, ain't it?"

Rose was jerked back into the present and Theo's eyes opened wide.

"Good heavens," he said. "Mrs Preston?"

"Arr. What you two doin' here, then?"

"Just having a look at the church, actually."

Mrs Preston's eyes went from Theo to Rose, whose hand was resting on his arm. "Nice church for a wedding, should you happen to be thinkin' of that," she said.

"Indeed," Theo said. "I have to ask, however, why you are cleaning it. Is this something you do regularly?"

"If I want to eat, I do."

"But I thought …" Rose began to say, and then stopped.

Their acquaintance with Mrs Preston dated back to the previous spring, and they had honestly never expected to see

8

her again. They had only met her because her husband had been murdered, and Theo had briefly been considered as a suspect. The late John Preston had been a bailiff, pursuing him for overdue rent on behalf of his employer, who owned the property Theo lived in.

The fact that Theo had been occupying two rather shabby rented rooms hadn't mattered to Preston's widow; in her eyes, anyone who wore a tailored suit must be a toff, and so she had christened him as such.

Eventually, John Preston's killer had been correctly identified and Theo's name completely cleared. Following that outcome, the man who had hired Preston had more or less guaranteed his widow an income for life, so it was puzzling that she would have to be scrubbing church floors in order to survive.

"You thought Mr Roscoe'd see me right?" she said.

"Well, yes," Rose said. "Or at least you wouldn't have to pay any rent for your rooms."

"Havin' the rent paid is one thing, but trouble is, you still got to eat and buy coal for the fire if you don't want to starve or freeze to death. So I decided to say 'thank you, but no thank you' to Mr Roscoe and go into service. Took a post with a lady by the name of Miss Irene Appleby. It's more work when you're in service, to be sure, but it's warm and you get meals, too."

So why had she lost what sounded like a reasonable post? Rose thought of her own small staff of servants, all of whom would be coming along with her after her marriage. Had the circumstances been different, they, too, could have lost their positions through no fault of their own.

"But you're obviously not with Miss Appleby now," Theo said. "What happened?"

For the first time, Mrs Preston's answer didn't come readily. Finally she said, "You two still lookin' into things for folks in trouble?"

"Yes, we are," Theo said slowly. One other result of his friendship with Rose had been the establishment of an investigative agency, yet another reason for her parents' disapproval. It had arisen directly from his involvement in the murder of John Preston, and Mrs Preston had considered herself their first client, paying the newly formed Milestone Investigative Agency the princely sum of two shillings for their help in finding her husband's killer.

But what on earth could that have to do with a domestic hiring?

"I'm still with Miss Appleby, but she ain't with me, so to speak."

"Where is she then?" Theo asked, hoping the answer wouldn't be "in her grave".

"She's havin' a spot of bother just now with that police inspector, the one you know."

"Inspector Reed?"

"That's the one. Thought he had some sense, but mebbe not."

Theo beckoned Mrs Preston to a pew. "Sit down and tell us what's going on. We may not be able to help, if that's what you had in mind, but I for one am completely mystified and I would like to know more."

Mrs Preston sat down with a muted grunt, which Rose attributed to her relief at being off her feet. Theo and Rose sat in the pew in front of her, turning to face her, and Theo folded his arms on the back of the pew.

"Start at the beginning, please. Who exactly is Miss Appleby?"

For some reason, Mrs Preston looked slightly embarrassed. "She's just a lady. Has a nice little house not far from here. St John Street."

"Elderly lady, is she?" Theo was picturing a spinster of advanced years, wanting a reliable servant to dust, scrub floors, clean grates and brush carpets. She'd prefer someone like Mrs Preston rather than a flighty young housemaid who would flirt with boot boys and delivery men.

"Elderly? Not her. Don't know exactly, but shouldn't think she's above thirty years at most. Probably less."

That was a bit puzzling, Rose had to admit. Assuming Miss Appleby was that young and unmarried, it was odd that she was not living with her parents, or if unfortunate enough to have lost both mother and father, with some other relation. The only possibility was that she had inherited enough money to set up her own household.

She could see from Theo's expression that he was thinking of something else.

"So how did Miss Appleby come to the attention of Inspector Reed? And how did that lead to you mopping the floor of this church?"

"That inspector," Mrs Preston said, "ain't got the brains he was born with. Anyone could see Miss Appleby had nothing to do with it."

"Nothing to do with what?" Theo asked patiently.

"That man bein' done to death. But that fool inspector thought she did and he came round a week or more ago with another copper and took her away. Said she was goin' to prison 'til he decided whether to charge her with murder."

"Oh, my goodness," Rose said.

"You may well say that. So there Miss Appleby is, sittin' in that prison cell waitin' to see if she's goin' on trial for her life, and me with no one to pay my wages. Who knows how long she might be there, so I come to the church to see if they could help me out. Vicar said I could do a bit of scrubbing here and he'd pay me for it. So there she is and here I am, and Lord knows what's goin' to happen to either of us."

Mrs Preston cast an eye at the altar as if a divine prediction on the subject might be forthcoming. It wasn't and she looked back at Theo and Rose.

"I know her and I'd swear she had nothing to do with it," she said.

"You're certain of that?" Rose asked gently. "Sometimes people do act out of character, if they're threatened or frightened."

"I know they do, but not her. I'd stake my life on it."

"You're fond of Miss Appleby, aren't you?" Theo said with a smile.

"She's all right." That was obviously high praise in Mrs Preston's view.

"But for Inspector Reed to arrest her, he must have had some proof that she was involved in the man's death. Who was he, by the way?"

For a moment, they thought she wasn't going to answer. But then her common sense must have kicked in; Theo and Rose couldn't offer any help or advice if they didn't even know whose death they were discussing.

"Man called Holt. Mr Timothy Holt."

"And what, if anything, was Mr Holt's connection with Miss Appleby?" Theo asked.

Again, there was an odd pause before she answered.

"S'pose you could call him her landlord, like, 'cept she don't pay no rent to live there."

Rose frowned, clearly puzzled, but Theo was much quicker to grasp what she was saying. He also assumed Mrs Preston wouldn't be offended on her employer's behalf if he was blunt about describing the relationship between the two.

"Are you saying that Miss Appleby was Mr Holt's mistress?"

Mrs Preston nodded. "Arr. And sittin' pretty with it, too, so why on earth would she ruin a good thing by killin' him?"

TWO

That was a good question, Theo had to admit. He knew two or three fairly wealthy men who kept mistresses and didn't begrudge the cost, being happy to pay rent and whatever other expenses arose in exchange for exclusive access to the woman in question. He wasn't acquainted with the female participants, but he assumed they were likewise satisfied with the arrangement.

Of course, there might be other parties involved in this case, for example, a Mrs Holt who was less than delighted to learn her husband was sleeping with another woman and financing a comfortable lifestyle for her. Or there might be other men vying for Miss Appleby's favors. It could even be that Irene Appleby had received a better offer from one of those men and Timothy Holt had refused to let her go.

Theo shot a glance at Rose, whose slightly pink cheeks couldn't be entirely blamed on the chill inside the church. He knew she wasn't so innocent as to be unaware of such relationships, but he supposed they weren't discussed over the teacups when she and her sisters or female friends got together.

And they certainly wouldn't be mentioned at all by Rose's mother, who usually pretended anything she disapproved of simply didn't exist.

It was clear that if the Milestone Agency were to be involved in Miss Appleby's dilemma at all, extreme tact and discretion would have to be employed.

"So you see," Mrs Preston said, "there weren't no reason for her to do him no harm. Fact is, I reckon she were rather fond of him. But the police – they don't believe her. They say she's just a jade, a dolly mop or whatever other name they can think of, and so she's bound to be lying."

Theo found it hard to believe Inspector Matthew Reed would have employed such language, although naturally, he had to enforce the law regarding prostitution. But Irene Appleby hadn't been working in a brothel or walking the streets of Oxford looking for customers. Neither did it seem likely she would have been involved in a pub brawl or picking the pockets of a man she'd entertained, both common reasons for prostitutes to end up in prison. The arrangement she had with Timothy Holt might be considered immoral, but it wasn't illegal.

"That's unfortunate," Theo said. "I'd have to ask, however, what you think Mrs Miles or I could do about her predicament. Because I feel sure that's what you were leading up to."

Mrs Preston gave him a look that indicated her low opinion of his intelligence.

"Well, if she didn't kill him, then somebody else did, didn't they? And if they've got her locked up, I don't reckon they're lookin' too hard to find out who it was. There's no one to speak up for her."

"We don't know Miss Appleby," Rose said. "You do, and you're convinced of her innocence, but what if you're wrong?"

"I'm not wrong."

It was clear Mrs Preston wasn't going to budge from her position and Theo sighed. He knew she was a fairly shrewd judge of character, as she had demonstrated during the investigation into her husband's murder. A better judge, in fact, than John Preston had been, since he had been imprudent enough to threaten the person who had subsequently killed him.

If she felt Irene Appleby hadn't killed her benefactor, she was probably correct. Unfortunately, she was also probably correct in that the police weren't going to stretch themselves too far to investigate further. They had a likely suspect, a woman of dubious morals in their view, so why look further?

Theo looked at Rose and got a tacit nod of approval. "I suppose we could ask a few questions and possibly see Miss Appleby," he said. "I assume she's allowed visitors?"

"Arr. I've been to see her twice, to take some clean linen and decent food. That dress they've made her wear in there ain't fit for rags, and the food … I wouldn't have fed nothin' like that to Preston. He'd have thrown it on the floor."

Theo had never been inside Oxford Prison, although he knew he had escaped imprisonment by the skin of his teeth. The building was forbidding enough from the outside, and he imagined the interior was just as grim, providing just the bare essentials for survival.

"That was kind of you," Rose said. "I'm sure she appreciated your thoughtfulness."

Mrs Preston shrugged off the compliment. "So you'll look into it? I ain't got much in the way of money, but if you prove she didn't kill him, Miss Appleby'd be sure to be grateful and she'd pay you."

"Even if she's now lost her source of income?" Theo inquired.

"Don't you worry about that. She ain't stupid, and I reckon she's got a bit put by."

And that was probably true, too. No kept woman was foolish enough to think the arrangement would last forever, and she would have no legal recourse whatsoever if the man decided to cut off her funds.

"As you may have gathered," Theo said, "Mrs Miles and I are planning to marry, and so we have other obligations at the moment, but I suppose we could make some preliminary inquiries. We know Inspector Reed, of course, and at least we may be able to hear his side of the story."

"Before we do anything, however," Rose said, "we need all the background information you can provide, and this is not really the best setting for that. Could you come to my house when you've finished here and we can discuss it further? Number 21, St Giles. I'll tell my butler to expect you."

Mrs Preston grinned. "Butler, eh? All right for some."

"He's not actually a butler, but he serves some of the functions of one," Rose said. "Anyway, I'll tell him you'll be coming by later."

"Ta. I'll do that. Piece of luck, weren't it, finding you two here? I was at my wits' ends tryin' to think of how to help Miss Appleby and then I saw you. Makes me think the Lord's lookin' after me, after all."

"It could be," Theo said. "We will speak further later, then."

They left Mrs Preston mopping with renewed energy and walked back toward Rose's house.

"Perhaps we shouldn't have committed ourselves to anything," Theo said. "You can chastise me if you wish, but I'd hate to see someone falsely convicted of murder, or even considered a suspect. If indeed, Miss Appleby is innocent of any wrong-doing. It's hard to form an opinion when we know nothing about her, or about her benefactor, for that matter."

"It sounds as if Inspector Reed isn't entirely convinced of her guilt if she hasn't been formally charged," Rose said. "I shan't chastise you. We can make a few inquiries and see what comes of it. After all, since the banns haven't been read yet, we have some time before the wedding."

"Yes, and we'll have to go back and corner the vicar to get that process started. In the meantime, we can await Mrs Preston's arrival with more information. We don't know, for example, when, where or how Mr Holt died. Essential details, as I think you'll agree."

"Absolutely. Theo, what if Miss Appleby is guilty? We can't prove her innocence if it doesn't exist."

"Then we can't, no matter how loyal Mrs Preston is. But I feel she is a reasonable judge of character, and she does have a point. One does not generally kill the goose – or in this case, the gander – who is providing the golden eggs."

"No, I suppose she wouldn't, unless the circumstances were quite unusual."

They had reached Rose's front door now, and Pickett opened it for them. As Rose had said, he was not exactly a butler, although he had more or less served that function since Edward's death. Previously he had been Edward's valet, and Rose imagined he was apprehensive about being relegated to that lesser role after she and Theo married. He was only serving as a butler-cum-bodyguard in the first place because Rose's parents had insisted she needed an extra layer of protection against unwanted intruders, although she had never rated his burglar-catching abilities very highly.

In any event, he had never had to chase one, had otherwise performed admirably, and Rose was content to let Theo decide what Pickett's duties would be in the future.

"We are expecting a caller later today, Pickett," Rose said. "Her name is Mrs Preston. I don't know what time she may call, but she is to be admitted."

"Yes, ma'am." Pickett was a good judge of social status, and quite capable of turning Mrs Preston away if not forewarned.

"She has a … friend … who may have been falsely accused of a serious crime," Theo said. "We are going to look into the matter on her behalf."

"Yes, sir," Pickett said, and Rose was sure she heard him sigh. Although Pickett had never actually confirmed this, she suspected he had been told to report back to her parents whether she was behaving properly, and establishing an investigative agency had been definitely improper. So was her habit of venturing out into Oxford's streets in pursuit of information, or taking on some imaginary role to corner a criminal.

However, Pickett was astute enough not to jeopardize his post, so he had compromised by fretting silently over Rose's participation whenever the agency had an active case and keeping the more dramatic details to himself.

He had also slowly come to accept Theo's role in her life and it seemed he had ultimately decided that if she was to marry a second time, it was just as well she was marrying someone who was capable of coping with her wilder impulses.

Rose's maid Cora took her hat and coat and they went into the drawing room where a glowing coal fire provided welcome warmth.

"We must be mad, planning a winter wedding," Theo said, holding his hands out to the fire. "Sensible people would have waited until summer, although I admit where you are concerned, any vestige of common sense on my part flies out the window. I wouldn't have wanted to wait until summer to marry."

"That's very flattering, Theo. But as you have pointed out on occasion, we shall meet with a certain amount of disapproval anyway, so the only difference between January and June is in the temperature."

"True, very true."

Rose rang for Cora and when she appeared, ordered tea for the two of them.

"We shall need a third cup when our new client arrives," she said. "Tell Cook we may want some small sandwiches, too."

"Yes, ma'am."

"That's a good idea," Theo said, when Cora had gone. "I wonder when's the last time Mrs Preston had a decent meal."

"Well, it sounded as though she is living in Miss Appleby's house and if there's a cook still, I imagine she's been able to have something to eat, even if it's not much as before. That won't last, however, if it was Mr Holt who was indirectly paying their wages and of course, he can't now, even if Miss Appleby is cleared of all involvement in his death. I'm not surprised Mrs Preston is worried about her future."

"Yes, going into service probably seemed a sound decision at the time. She could hardly predict Miss Appleby's protector being murdered. I wonder what exactly happened to him?"

"No doubt we will be told. Thank you, Cora." Rose poured two cups of tea from the tray provided and Theo took one.

"I confess I am curious to meet Miss Appleby," he said, "although I doubt she will be at her best when I do. Prison is not a congenial environment."

"I shouldn't think it is. If she is indeed innocent, she must be very frightened, wondering what will happen if she can't prove she didn't kill Mr Holt. Will she be allowed a solicitor, or barrister?"

"Not unless charges are actually brought, I think. So time is of the essence, and of course, we must try and establish why Reed thinks she is guilty. Lack of any other suspects, do you think? Or just because the police believe a woman of easy virtue – or whatever term they use – must be lying?"

Rose nodded. "That's what Mrs Preston said, wasn't it? I can't say I approve of their arrangement, but that doesn't mean she should be accused falsely because of it."

"That's a compassionate attitude," Theo said, "and one we shall have to maintain, rather than being at all judgemental. After all, Irene Appleby may turn out to be very charming."

"I wonder why Mr Holt didn't marry her," Rose mused. "Do you think he was already married?"

"That is often the case. Or she may be from a very humble background and he felt that she wouldn't be socially acceptable as his wife. If he could afford to pay all her expenses, he must have had a reasonable income and position in society."

Rose was quiet and Theo was sure she was running through a mental checklist of all the people she had heard of in the upper layers of Oxford society. Personally, he had never heard of Timothy Holt, but that meant nothing. The man might not even have lived in Oxford, only visiting occasionally to see Irene Appleby. Finally she shook her head.

"I don't remember ever hearing his name," she said. "Let's hope Mrs Preston knows something about him, or this will be difficult."

"It will be difficult anyway if he was married," Theo said with a grin. "I don't fancy going to the house of a bereaved widow and asking if she knows her late husband had a young mistress."

"Oh, I imagine she knew," Rose said, "but a well-bred lady would never mention the fact, even to her closest friends. And certainly not to her husband. Of course, we may be wrong and Mr Holt may not have been married."

"Let's hope not." Theo cocked his head. "Is that someone at the front door?"

It was, and they heard Pickett calmly asking their caller her name before letting her inside and opening the drawing room door.

"Mrs Preston, ma'am."

Mrs Preston had tidied herself up for the visit, they saw, discarding the apron and mob cap and wearing what was undoubtedly her best dress and coat, a neat bonnet tied under her chin. Theo stood up when she entered, a gesture of courtesy that brought a look of surprise and then amusement from their client.

Rose said, "Do come in and sit by the fire. It's bitter outside, isn't it?"

"It is that." Mrs Preston crossed the room and sat gingerly in an armchair near the fire.

"May I offer you a cup of tea?"

"That'd be welcome." She looked at Theo. "Sit down, then. You make me twitchy, standing there."

Theo chuckled and sat down. Rose rang again for Cora, who shot Mrs Preston one curious look and then disappeared into the kitchen to fetch the tea.

"If we are going to help Miss Appleby, we need to know any bit of information, however small, that may be relevant," Theo said. "And you must be honest with us. Trying to protect her, or her reputation, won't be helpful."

"I know that."

"Good. Here comes Cora with the tea, so we'll have that first and then you can tell us what happened."

Cook had fulfilled Rose's order, and there were small triangular sandwiches and thin slices of ginger cake on the tea tray along with a freshly filled teapot and a third cup and saucer. Mrs Preston's eyes widened and they could see her struggling between hunger and a desire not to be thought greedy.

She compromised by taking two small sandwiches and a slice of cake. Theo and Rose followed suit, hoping that would make her feel comfortable enough to share any information she possessed.

When the food had disappeared and Rose had refilled the teacups, Theo said, "I hope to visit Miss Appleby and make my own assessment of her, but of course, I can't call on Mr Holt. We can fill in the background on his life later; first please tell us anything you know about his death."

Mellowed by the food and the warmth of the fire, Mrs Preston settled back in her chair.

"'Twas a fortnight ago, near enough," she said. "The Wednesday, it was. He'd come to see her in the afternoon, like he usually did."

"A daily occurrence?" Theo asked.

"Lord, no. Once or twice a week, mebbe. Sometimes not even that. He just wanted her to be there whenever he wanted to call on her."

Theo thought it was very generous of Timothy Holt to be paying the bills for a mistress he visited only occasionally. Perhaps it was more than simply a financial arrangement; he might have genuinely loved her.

"And how long had this arrangement been in place, do you know?"

"Not for certain, but I've been in service there almost six months and it weren't anything new. So a year or more, I'd think."

"It was a well-established routine, then. When he called that day, how did he arrive? On foot?"

"Weren't going to walk all the way from St Clements, was he, 'specially in winter? Maybe walked the last bit, but most of the way in a hansom cab."

Theo's parents lived not far from St Clements, and he made a mental note to ask his mother if she knew anything about Timothy Holt.

"Then what happened?"

Mrs Preston gave him a scornful look. "What usually happens when a man calls on a lady he's paying for."

Rose blushed and Theo said, "That's not exactly what I meant. What were the circumstances of his death? Did he die in Miss Appleby's house?"

"No, he did not. Left on his own two feet, he did. I was in the kitchen and I seen him go."

"Go where? Just out of the house, or to hail a cab, or what?"

"He walked down to the corner. Didn't see what happened after that, but I reckon he went to Beaumont Street to get a cab."

Rose was frowning. "So when did he meet his death? If he was alive and fit when he left Miss Appleby …"

"Them coppers said that when he got back to his own house in the cab, he didn't get out, so the driver went to open the door to see why and he found Mr Holt were dead. Stabbed, they reckoned, being as there was blood all over the seat, and him half fallin' off it."

"But no weapon was found?"

"No, and nobody else in the cab either. So you tell me, how did he get stabbed to death when there weren't nothing to stab him with and no one to do it?"

THREE

"A good question," Theo said. "Of course, that assumes the cab driver is telling the truth and no one else got in or out of the cab during the trip."

Mrs Preston shrugged her shoulders. "No reason for him to lie about it. He ain't got a dog in this fight."

"And I suppose the police questioned him at length."

"Far as I know."

Theo knew he could check with Inspector Reed, but he was certain the cab driver would have been thoroughly interrogated. He did wonder what the man's reaction would have been upon reaching the destination and discovering that his passenger was dead, and what was more, had left the interior of the cab looking like an abattoir.

Shock and disgust, probably, along with irritation that he'd lost the fare and would have to spend the next hour or more answering questions from the police. And then the cab would have to be thoroughly cleaned before he could use it again. It was safe to say that if he knew who was responsible, he'd have had no qualms about relaying that to the police.

"Tell me," Rose said, "how did Miss Appleby learn of Mr Holt's death? If he was alive and well when he left her, someone must have known of their relationship to be able to inform her. I wouldn't have thought the police would simply turn up on her doorstep if they didn't know about it."

Theo looked at her admiringly, since he hadn't thought of that. If the arrangement was meant to be a secret, then it hadn't been as secret as either party had assumed.

Mrs Preston thought about it, wrinkling her forehead.

"Reckon it were the cab driver. I heard them talkin' about it once, her and Mr Holt. It was only a hansom cab, not his own carriage or nothin', but I think he had that same driver bringin' him and takin' him back more'n once. So when the police started askin' about where he'd got his fare, he probably thought he'd better tell 'em."

"But it sounds as though he didn't deliver Mr Holt to her door or collect him there," Rose objected. "The cab ride both ways may have been only as far as Beaumont Street. Would the driver have known exactly where Mr Holt was going?"

"He might not have done, but someone would," Mrs Preston said. "People snoop and they talk, don't they? Wouldn't take too much to find someone who saw him goin' to her door or comin' from it, even if the driver didn't."

And that was probably true, too. Neighbors, servants and street urchins all would have been questioned, any one of whom might have seen Holt at Miss Appleby's house. Since it was a regular occurrence, that made it even more likely he had been observed. It wouldn't take a diligent constable – or inspector – very long to identify Holt's destination, once they had the corner of Beaumont Street and St John Street as a starting point..

"And it also sounds as though the driver wasn't simply an accidental, random participant, if he'd taken him there more than once," Theo said. "Do you happen to know his name?"

"No."

So that was another piece of information to be obtained from the police, Theo thought, because he had no intention of trying to track down one cab driver from among the dozens who plied their trade on the streets of Oxford. Admittedly, there couldn't be too many who'd had a passenger murdered in their cab recently, but he preferred to cut corners and save time where possible.

"There's another possibility besides the driver," Rose said, a little reluctantly. "If Mr Holt was married, his wife may well have known about Miss Appleby and where she could be found. Just because she didn't say anything to others doesn't mean she was unaware of the liaison."

"S'pose not," Mrs Preston said.

"Was a wife ever mentioned?" Theo asked.

"Not in my hearing."

She looked a little embarrassed at this, and Theo assumed it was because she had eavesdropped on their conversations whenever possible. Servants often did, even though their employers tended to ignore the fact that their staff had ears, eyes and a strong sense of curiosity. However, an equally strong sense of self-preservation generally kept them from saying much about what they'd observed or overheard.

"That doesn't mean there wasn't one. You knew Mr Holt came from St Clements; how did you learn that?"

"Heard him sayin' something about it," Mrs Preston said, confirming their suspicion she had been listening avidly to any scraps of overheard conversation. "And that's where he was goin' in that cab, weren't he? Else he wouldn't have been found when it got there."

Theo had to admit she had cornered him on that fact.

"Very well, tell us what else you know about him. Start with a description, please."

"What good will that do? The man's dead. You won't see him walkin' around anywhere."

"It might help to know where he may have been seen other than at Miss Appleby's house."

"Oh." Mrs Preston closed her eyes for a moment, possibly visualizing the late Timothy Holt. "He was older'n her, maybe forty or a bit more, a tall, thin fellow. Always real serious-looking, but polite, like, with light blue eyes like he was looking right through you."

"Smartly dressed?"

Mrs Preston's eyes roamed over Theo's well-tailored three-piece suit. "Arr, a toff, like you."

"Did he speak to you?"

"A few words, now and again. He talked posh, too, like you. And Mrs Miles," she added, giving Rose an approving look.

Theo met Rose's eyes and couldn't help smiling. Speech was always a good way of identifying one's place in society, and as it happened, his family's thriving brewery business meant Theo and his brothers had been sent to a decent school to acquire a good education. Rose, he knew, had shared a governess with her sisters, and would have had good grammar and diction drummed into her from an early age.

Mrs Preston, on the other hand, had probably never been inside a schoolroom, and they would have been surprised if she could read and write beyond a very basic level, if that.

"Have you any idea of Mr Holt's profession or the source of his income?" he asked.

"No, I do not. Why would he tell the likes of me? Most interestin' thing he ever said to me was whether it were raining or not."

"But it's possible Miss Appleby may have mentioned it," Rose said. "Did she?"

"Not to me."

Theo decided to abandon Timothy Holt for the time being, since he now had a rough sketch of the man's appearance and personality. A serious man in his forties, highly respectable aside from his association with Miss Appleby. A man of independent means, since he could afford not only to pay her bills, but take time during the day to visit her.

And he had taken a certain amount of precaution in doing that. He had used an anonymous hansom cab every time, not always the same one, and not been taken all the way to her door. That suggested he wanted to keep the liaison secret. Holt was hardly the first man to take a mistress, so why was he concerned? To protect his reputation, or because he feared the consequences if it were to become known? Or just possibly, to protect Irene Appleby.

"Very well, now it's time to learn a bit more about Miss Appleby," Theo said. "If I'm to see her, I'd like to know something of her background first. Can you help us there?"

Mrs Preston shook her head reluctantly. "I don't know much about that. She said once she'd lived in Oxford all her life, but then so have lots of folks. She never said anything about a ma or pa or any other family, so mebbe she was an orphan, left to make her own way in the world. If that's true, you can't blame her for bein' happy to pleasure Mr Holt if he was willin' to pay for her to live there."

That was a distinct possibility. It was understandable that a young woman with no resources other than her looks and personality would use those to avoid a life of servitude or worse. Being offered a house and a reasonable way of life would outweigh any moral considerations for most young women who found themselves in that situation, and was definitely an improvement over prostitution, begging, going into service or back-breaking factory work.

Of course, there were plenty who would still blame her, undoubtedly those who would never find themselves faced with that sort of moral dilemma.

"You're a good judge of character, Mrs Preston," Rose said, aiming for a matter-of-fact tone rather than blatant flattery. "Do you think she worried at all about her reputation being compromised?"

"Doubt it. Oh, she weren't braggin' about it," Mrs Preston said hastily, "But she weren't ashamed neither. You do what you have to do, don't you?"

"I expect so," Theo said. "It sounds as though they both benefitted from the arrangement. Now, who else was living in the house? Other servants? A cook, or lady's maid?"

"There's a cook and lady's maid both, and I don't mind tellin' you all three of us are worried sick about Miss Appleby. Not just 'cause of mebbe losing our posts but … well, it ain't right for her to be in jail over something she didn't do. That's why I come to you."

Irene Appleby sounded like a considerate employer, to inspire such loyalty in her servants, Theo thought. Perhaps they recognized a kindred spirit, if she had come from an equally humble background.

"Do the other two know you're here?" he asked.

"Not as such. I just said I was going to talk to someone who might help her."

"And did they approve?"

"Course they did."

"As I said, we can't promise anything," Theo said. "But we will see what we can do. Now, on the day Mr Holt died, where was Miss Appleby after he'd left the house? Did she go out at all?"

"She went to the milliner's not long afterwards," Mrs Preston said. "Wish she hadn't done, 'cause the police reckon she didn't really go there. They said she must have caught up with him somewhere and stabbed him to death. Course they didn't bother to say why she'd have done that."

"Does the milliner confirm that she was there?" Rose asked. "For example, did she buy or order a hat that day?"

"I don't know."

"You'd have thought the police would have checked that. Where is the millinery?"

"Little Clarendon Street. Not far. Five minutes' walk, mebbe."

"Would she have walked there?"

"Far as I know. She'd been there before and walked."

"How long was it before she returned home?" Theo asked.

Mrs Preston cocked her head on one side and considered. "She were back well before tea. So mebbe half an hour or a bit longer."

"And she seemed as normal when she returned?"

"Didn't look like she'd just stabbed someone to death, if that's what you mean."

"If she did walk to the millinery in Little Clarendon Street," Rose said, "that is in the opposite direction from the way Mr Holt went in the hansom cab. I imagine I could call in and discover whether she actually did go to the shop that day."

"And if she did," Mrs Preston said with an air of triumph, "she couldn't have been doing Mr Holt to death at the same time."

"Assuming he was going straight back to St Clements," Theo said. "But yes, it would be something to support Miss Appleby's claim of innocence. I can't somehow see Mr Holt calling in at a ladies' millinery on his way home. If he wanted to buy a new hat for her, surely he would have merely given her the money for it."

"You'd think so, since ladies like to choose their own hats," Rose said. She knew she did, and was looking forward to being able to wear something other than an unbecoming black bonnet once she and Theo had married. Something sedate and appropriate, naturally, but not … black.

She dragged her thoughts back to the present.

"Very well, that is perhaps something I can confirm," she said. "Mr Stone will speak to Inspector Reed and then arrange to visit Miss Appleby at the prison."

Mrs Preston looked from one to the other. "That's real kind of you both," she said. "Why d'ye do this sort of thing, anyway? I know why you was mixed up in it when Preston was killed, but other folks' business … well, it ain't nothing to you, is it? Can't think you're gettin' rich off it."

Theo grinned at her. "Hardly. I suppose because it is satisfying to be able to help someone, especially when they've been falsely accused. As you so rightly say, I know how that feels – a combination of fear and anger, compounded by helplessness – although fortunately I was never actually thrown into prison. So we will make some inquiries and see how the land lies."

"I don't want her hanged for something she didn't do."

"No, course not. Nor do you want the true criminal to escape justice."

"Too right, Mr Stone."

It was one of the few times she had called him by his name, and Theo was touched.

"We'll do our best, Mrs Preston."

"And you'll tell me how it's going?"

"Yes, we will do. I expect you'll be at the church, so we'll find you there when we have something to report. What's the number of Miss Appleby's house in St John Street, by the way? We may want to speak to the cook or maid."

"Number nine." She heaved herself to her feet. "I'll be off then, and let you get on with it. Ta for the tea and sandwiches. Right tasty, those were."

"I'm glad you enjoyed them," Rose said. She rang for Pickett, who materialized so quickly that she suspected he'd been listening at the keyhole. If he had, it would be interesting to see what he had made of Irene Appleby's way of life and subsequent incarceration. She hoped he wouldn't take the attitude that it served her right.

Theo accompanied them to the front door and when it had closed, he returned to the drawing room.

"Have we got ourselves embroiled in something unsavory, do you think?" he asked Rose. "I'd certainly like to believe Mrs Preston, but there may be factors we – and she – are not aware of. Obviously her knowledge is bound to be a bit limited, since both parties appear to have been reasonably discreet."

"I, for one, would like to know more about Mr Holt," Rose said. "Most importantly, if he is married and whether his wife knew about Miss Appleby."

"I think he must be married; why else would he skulk around like that to see a mistress?"

"I bow to your superior knowledge on that subject," Rose said, her eyes twinkling.

"Not that you will ever have cause to be concerned. I would also like to know what his source of income is. He must have considerable resources to be able to support Miss Appleby as well as a wife and family, and we are assuming he has them."

"Yes, that would be useful. Speaking of income, Theo, I notice you didn't enlighten Mrs Preston as to the other reason we have taken on some of our cases. Or should I say, the secondary result of the outcomes."

"My books, you mean."

"Yes."

Theo was still marveling over the transformation in his personal finances, once he had abandoned his unsuccessful efforts to write serious literature and instead, had turned the Preston case into a highly fictionalized novel. The public had lapped it up, and the delighted publisher had commissioned Theo to keep churning out similar titles.

The inspiration for the plots had largely come from the real-life cases the Milestone Agency had taken on, including the book he was currently writing, titled *Honesty for Sale*. All he had to do was make sure no one involved in the real cases could recognize themselves in the pages of his novels.

The resultant income had given him the courage to propose to Rose, even though he knew her mother was appalled that her daughter was marrying an author whose work could best be described as sensational. To be marrying the son of a brewery owner was bad enough, but this was far worse.

Rose, however, heartily approved and had read all the books he had written so far with a sense of amusement and pride. Theo was a talented writer, she felt, and since the reading public bought and enjoyed his works, why shouldn't he continue to produce them?

Even Theo's father, who had been disappointed that his eldest son hadn't followed him into the family business, had to admit he was now making good on his ambition to support himself through writing.

"I doubt Mrs Preston will ever read any of them, which is probably just as well," Theo said. "It's entirely possible she can't read or write at all. And I doubt we will turn much of a profit on this matter, despite any money Miss Appleby may have tucked away for a rainy day."

"Do you think she has done that?"

"I wouldn't be at all surprised. But should we be able to rescue her from a false accusation of murder and at the same time identify the true killer, we will not only feel a warm glow of satisfaction at seeing justice done, but I shall have the raw material for another book."

FOUR

The first order of business, they agreed, was to return to the vicarage and arrange for the marriage banns to be read at Holy Trinity. This had to be done on the three Sundays before the wedding, meaning they could plan to be married in February.

"A miserable month," Theo observed, when they had consulted the vicar and received his approval. "I'm only glad there will be something in February to look forward to this year. And every year afterwards, as we mark our wedding anniversary."

"I do like the way you always find something to be positive about," Rose said. "I fret too much about things going wrong."

"Nothing will go wrong with us, my dear."

"No, but that's not exactly what I meant. It's hard to explain, but you have a way of turning things around which I quite admire. An irrepressible optimism, if you will."

"Such as being optimistic enough to approach a young lady I had never met and expecting her to help me evade a bailiff?"

"Something like that, yes." Rose tucked her hand into the crook of his elbow and smiled up at him, remembering the day they had met.

"And look what resulted from that. So I will leave the details of organizing the wedding to you, unless you wish to consult me, and I will make a start on determining exactly what happened when Timothy Holt departed this vale of tears. I think consulting Inspector Reed will be the first task."

"And whilst you are doing that, I shall see about ordering a new hat, since the millinery in Little Clarendon Street came so highly recommended by an acquaintance of mine."

"Just as long as the milliner doesn't think your domestic arrangement is similar to Miss Appleby's," Theo said. "I admit she may not have been aware of it, and only thinking of a potential sale, but as Mrs Preston so rightly observed, people snoop and they gossip."

"I shall be a model of rectitude," Rose said.

"As you always are. I, on the other hand, will be spending much of the afternoon in the police station. Not the most salubrious venue, but necessary."

Theo offered to accompany Rose to the millinery before going off to consult Inspector Reed, a gesture she was willing to accept. While Little Clarendon Street wasn't far away, she still felt uneasy about venturing onto the streets without an escort. She sometimes thought she must have been mad to take the walk which had resulted in meeting Theo. As he had observed, the outcome had been worth it, but it could have ended much differently.

So she was obscurely grateful as they walked down St Giles and turned into Little Clarendon Street, a short lane lined with shops, including the millinery. Rose peered in the window, noting that the hats and bonnets on display were well-made and the latest fashion.

"Those are quite charming," she said. "I know I am here under somewhat false pretences, but I still may indulge myself by buying a new hat."

"You certainly may, if you wish," Theo said. "Shall I wait outside for you?"

Rose hesitated. "No, I don't think you need to. It's only a few minutes' walk back to the house, and it's broad daylight. I shall be perfectly all right."

"If you're certain."

"Yes, go ahead and speak to Inspector Reed."

Theo watched her go into the millinery, and then turned reluctantly to go back toward St Giles. He had a longer walk to get to the police station, and no guarantee that Reed would be in, or that he would share any information with Theo if he was.

Rose opened the door of the millinery, setting a bell jingling, although there was actually no need since the proprietor was on the shop floor and came forward to greet her. Her eyes swept over Rose's coat and hat – black, but expensive – and registered approval. This was a potential customer who might spend a reasonable amount of money, and so should be treated accordingly.

For her part, Rose smiled courteously, feeling that the milliner might be a possible source of useful information.

"Good afternoon, madam," the woman said. "May I be of service?"

"Good afternoon. I do hope so; I am in search of a hat to wear to a wedding."

"But of course. I would be pleased to show you several that would be suitable."

Rose noted that the woman assumed she would be a guest at the wedding, not the bride. She supposed that was logical, since she was still wearing a long black coat and bonnet, with black gloves on her hands.

"As it happens," she confided, "I am to be married before long. A second wedding, as I am a widow, so I wish to wear something … tasteful."

The milliner didn't bat an eye at this scandalous behavior on Rose's part.

"I am sure we can find a suitable hat for you to wear, madam. May I ask where the wedding is to be?"

"Holy Trinity Church." She gave the milliner a conspiratorial smile. "A small church, for a quiet wedding."

"I understand completely. Let me show you some possibilities."

Rose nearly forgot she was supposed to be gathering information about Irene Appleby as the milliner brought out half a dozen hats, each one more attractive than the last. None of them were overly flashy or likely to cause clucks of disapproval from anyone observing them. In fact, Rose thought, even her mother could find little to criticize about them.

"These are lovely," she said. "I especially like this one."

She touched a hat in a soft silvery gray color that reminded her of catkins on willow trees, one of the first signs of spring each year. Gray was very appropriate – a step away from black but still somber and dignified.

"Would madam care to try it?"

"Yes, please."

Rose removed her black bonnet and settled the gray hat on her head. It could have been made for her; fitting perfectly and framing her face without overwhelming it.

"Oh, I do like this one. Yes, I'll have it. Would you be kind enough to put it aside for me?"

"Certainly, madam. And may I say it is an excellent choice. Very appropriate for a small, intimate wedding."

"I will come back later and collect it, if I may." She gave the milliner a warm smile. "Miss Appleby was certainly correct when she said this millinery was a delightful place to shop. And the hats are beautiful."

"I am pleased to hear that she recommended us."

"Oh, yes. I understand she comes here quite often."

"She is a regular customer, yes, or at least she used to be."

Alarm bells went off in Rose's mind. "Used to be? I believe she called in here less than a fortnight ago. The Wednesday, I think she said."

The milliner shook her head. "Miss Appleby must be thinking of another shop. She hasn't been in for at least a month, perhaps a bit more. I wish she would, however; she has excellent taste."

And a fair amount of money to spend on fripperies like stylish hats, Rose thought. No wonder the milliner hoped she would return.

"Well, I am sure she would not purchase a hat anywhere else, having this millinery to hand, so perhaps she was referring to something else. Or I may be mistaken as to the date. No matter. Thank you so much for your help, and I shall come to collect the hat before the end of the week."

"Very good, madam."

Rose noticed that she hadn't been asked for her name, not that she was going to volunteer that information. It was taken for granted that an affluent customer would keep her word and return to collect and pay for the hat she had chosen. A lady wouldn't carry cash with her and Rose didn't have an account with the shop, so the milliner probably assumed she would have to get the cost of the hat from a male source. She chuckled at the thought of asking Theo to pay for it, even though she knew he wouldn't mind.

She gave the milliner a last smile and left the shop, pleased to have found a suitable hat, but disturbed as to the other aspect of her visit. She and Theo were proceeding on the assumption that Irene Appleby was telling the truth when she denied having anything to do with Timothy Holt's death, and it was disconcerting to learn she had lied about where she'd been at roughly the same time as he was being stabbed to death.

If she had been counting on the milliner to give her an alibi, she would be mistaken. Or had she indeed started out for the millinery and then been side-tracked? She could have ended up somewhere else, either voluntarily or because someone else had intervened.

Rose had intended to go directly back to her house, but since she was so close to St John Street, she decided to make a short detour and see what the house looked like that Timothy Holt had so generously provided for Irene Appleby.

A few minutes' walk took her to the address in question. Rose didn't pause in front of it but simply walked past, noting that it was situated at the end of a short terrace of similar brick houses, with nothing to distinguish it. Light blue curtains hung in the two front windows and the front step had been recently scrubbed, probably by Mrs Preston.

In short, it was a small, tidy house, suitable for a young woman and her domestic staff. The three servants would probably occupy rooms in the attic, while Miss Appleby slept in a bedroom on the floor below. There would be a kitchen, parlor and small scullery on the ground floor and possibly a tiny garden at the rear of the property.

Rose turned at the next street, making her way back toward St Giles. Where could Irene Appleby have gone if not to the millinery? There were other shops in Little Clarendon Street, so perhaps she had decided to call in there rather than look at hats. Or perhaps she had gone in another direction altogether, which would complicate things immensely.

There was no way of knowing, and Rose was not about to start querying local shop owners whether they had seen her on the day in question. Better to let Theo put the question to her directly when he saw her in prison and see what she had to say.

She walked up St Giles and turned in at her own house, pretending not to notice Pickett's obvious relief that she had returned unharmed from the perilous streets of Oxford. Rose was willing to concede there might be dangers lurking there on occasion, but she rather resented Pickett thinking she couldn't get from the millinery to her house without losing her way or being attacked.

Cora took her coat and bonnet and Rose said, "I have ordered a new hat to wear at the wedding, Cora. A soft gray, which I think will be quite suitable."

"It sounds lovely, ma'am."

Cora was relieved that Rose was re-marrying, partly because she had sympathized with her frustration during the period of mourning, and also because that meant there was now no chance of Rose being forced to move back and live with her parents. That had been a frequent threat after Edward's death, and Cora had no wish to be taking orders from Rose's mother.

"I admit it will be pleasant to wear something besides black."

"Yes, ma'am, it surely will do."

Cora had been almost as distressed as her mistress at the sight of a wardrobe filled with colorful, fashionable dresses that she had been forbidden to wear after Edward's death. A gray hat to be worn in public was a small but welcome step back to normality.

"So I think I will have a cup of tea now. Mr Stone will be by later, after he's been to see Inspector Reed."

"Beggin' your pardon, ma'am, but has that to do with that … lady … who was here earlier?"

"Yes, it is. We are trying to find out whether her mistress has been falsely accused of killing a man."

Cora's eyes grew wide. "Oh, my goodness. I hope you and Mr Stone find out, if she didn't do it."

"So do I," Rose said. "but I think it may be more difficult than we first thought."

If Theo had heard her say that, he would have heartily agreed. He was seated in the Oxford police station at the time, trying to pry information from the inspector. Normally, Theo was fairly adept at getting people to talk, but in Matthew Reed he had met his match.

The inspector was not impressed to hear that the Milestone Agency was looking into the case, and for his part, Theo didn't particularly want to remind the inspector of the Preston case by revealing that the request had come from Mrs Preston. So he had compromised by saying that he had learned Miss Appleby's servants were very concerned that she was being detained in connection with the death of a man she had no reason to have wished dead.

"Because I should think you would need to prove a motive," Theo said. "Not only was he providing financial security for her, but her servants say she was quite fond of him. That's two good reasons for her to want him alive."

Reed gave him a critical glance. "You know as well as I, Mr Stone, that sort of arrangement is rarely permanent. She may have found a more generous benefactor. He may have tired of her."

"But there is no indication that either of those things happened."

"They would hardly announce it to the world," Reed said. "A man keeping a mistress does not, in my experience, let anyone but perhaps a brother or close friends know what he is doing, and the woman in question is not going to tell him if she receives a better offer."

"And did Mr Holt tell any brothers or close friends about his paramour?"

"Not that we have yet discovered. You will appreciate that I have had to exercise a great deal of tact in my questioning."

"I do indeed appreciate that, Inspector. Particularly in regard to Mrs Holt, I imagine." Reed frowned at him and Theo added, "There *is* a Mrs Holt, isn't there?"

"Why do you say that?"

"Because I assume that if the liaison was not something to be kept secret from a wife, he wouldn't have taken the precaution of not having the hansom take him directly to her door."

"How did ... oh, the servants."

"Yes. I also assume you have spoken to her, tactfully, of course."

"I have done. She is of the opinion some ruffian knifed her husband."

Theo raised his eyebrows. "A ruffian in a cab with Mr Holt as the only passenger?"

"It is possible the wound was inflicted before he got into the cab. In fact, that is the only logical explanation, since the cab driver swears no one else got in or out of it during the journey, and no weapon was found there."

"So one assumes the attacker either took it away with them or disposed of it as soon as possible. And Mr Holt slowly bled to death during the ride to his home."

"So it would seem."

"Did he say anything to the driver to indicate he was suffering from such a wound?"

"No."

"And the driver noticed nothing amiss?"

"He says not."

"And no likely assailant was glimpsed on the street when Mr Holt hailed the cab?"

"Not that we have found. You will appreciate the difficulty in finding witnesses once the event is past."

"Do you believe the driver is being entirely truthful?"

"Let us say," Reed said, "there is no reason at present to suspect him of lying."

"Would you be willing to give me his name? Not that I think you haven't been thorough in questioning him, but he may have belatedly thought of something he didn't mention at the time."

Reed sighed, and Theo hoped he would be given the name simply because the inspector wanted to be rid of him.

"His name is William Bellamy, and should you decide to harass him, which I cannot legally prevent you from doing, please remember we do not suspect him of any collusion in Mr Holt's death."

"So why have you assumed Miss Appleby was responsible? Was she seen wiping blood from a sharp kitchen knife at the time?"

"I'd advise you not to be too flippant, Mr Stone," the inspector said. "Is Miss Appleby your client?"

"Only indirectly. But I do want to know, if you will tell me, why you suspect her, other than a vague theory that she might have wanted revenge if he was about to end their affair. Frankly, I would have been more inclined to think she would try to charm her way back into favor, if that were the case, rather than kill him."

"I suspect her because I have no more likely candidate. She has provided no alibi for the time in question and she could have a reason to want him dead that we know nothing about."

"And so could other people."

Theo was somewhat alarmed to hear himself defending Irene Appleby so vehemently. After all, he had never met the woman and was relying solely on Mrs Preston's character analysis. He decided not to mention the visit she had made to the millinery, although he wondered why she hadn't told the police about it. That would have given her an alibi, or at least thrown reasonable doubt on her involvement.

"That is possible," Reed said, "and if so, I hope Miss Appleby will help us identify them, if only to save her own neck."

"You haven't charged her with anything yet, have you?"

"Not yet, no."

Theo cleared his throat. "Would it be possible for me to see her and speak to her, Inspector? It could be that if she realizes I am trying to clear her name, she will be more forthcoming than she has been with you."

Reed thought this over for so long that Theo was sure he was going to turn down the request. But finally he said, "Very well. On one condition."

"Yes?"

"That you immediately report back to me anything that would advance this case, whether it is to Miss Appleby's benefit or not. After all, you tell me she is not actually your client."

It took Theo only a second to make up his mind.

"No, she is not, but I would hate to see a miscarriage of justice, and I am sure you would agree. So I accept your terms. When will I be able to see her?"

FIVE

"You can go tomorrow, I should think," Reed said.

"And will I be able to speak to her on my own? I think she would be more honest if there wasn't a warden or police officer hovering nearby."

"Don't press your luck, Mr Stone," Reed warned. "I will have Bennett accompany you, but he can wait just out of earshot whilst you speak to Miss Appleby."

"Thank you; that will do admirably."

Theo was familiar with Sergeant Bennett, who frequently worked with Reed. He was a stolid, honest man with no particular ax to grind, and was probably uneasy about locking up a young woman who hadn't been proven to commit a crime, regardless of his opinion of her morals. Of course, he wouldn't voice that doubt to his superior, but he might to Theo.

"Very well. If you will go to the prison tomorrow at ten in the morning, I will have Bennett meet you and escort you inside. You may have fifteen minutes of conversation with Irene Appleby, and as I said, anything of use you learn must be reported back to me. Or to Bennett, who will then tell me. Is that clear?"

"Absolutely." Theo had hoped for a longer session, but it was obvious fifteen minutes was all he was going to get. With luck, he might be able to arrange a second visit on another day.

"Is there anything else?"

"I don't believe so. Thank you for being so helpful, Inspector."

They shook hands and Theo left the station, reflecting that he had been at least partially successful. He could see Irene Appleby the next day and form his own opinion of her guilt or innocence. And with any luck, she might reveal information that would move the case forward. If she was not guilty, she might be helpful in identifying who was, and if she *had* stabbed Holt …

Theo spared a moment to think what his reaction would be if he discovered she had actually killed the man funding her lifestyle. It seemed unlikely, but as Rose had pointed out, people who were being threatened or were frightened might do something completely at odds with their usual character. Until he met and spoke with Irene Appleby, he would have no idea if that was possible in this instance. And he would have to do that in the space of fifteen minutes.

So his emotions were mixed as he walked through the center of Oxford and emerged on the far side, where the bustling Cornmarket street gave way to Magdalen Street and then the calmer St Giles, and shops began to be replaced by private residences.

By the time he reached Rose's house, he had mentally prepared a few questions to put to Irene Appleby, with follow-up ones, depending on her responses. He only hoped she wouldn't refuse to speak to him at all, but he couldn't see that happening. A young woman possibly facing a murder trial, and the gallows if she couldn't sway a jury, would hardly turn down an offer of help. Especially if she was innocent. Or so Theo reasoned.

"Were you successful, Theo?" Rose asked, when he was seated by the fire .

"At least partially. I am to see Miss Appleby tomorrow morning, accompanied by Sergeant Bennett. Inspector Reed was not overjoyed to learn we are involved, possibly because it seems he has no compelling reason to accuse her of the crime. It seems more a case of lacking anyone more likely."

Rose's face was serious and Theo said, "What happened at the millinery? You don't look like someone who has uncovered evidence to help our client."

"No, I'm not." Rose related the milliner's comment that Irene hadn't called in at the shop for at least a month.

"Of course, she may be wrong about the time frame, and I hope she is. But she seemed very sure about it. If so, that means either that Miss Appleby lied about where she'd gone, or she somehow was prevented from going there."

"However, that would explain why she didn't offer that alibi to the police," Theo said. "I did wonder about that. She knew it would be checked and found to be false."

"Yes. Where do you suppose she went? She obviously left the house to go somewhere, since the servants saw her leave."

"I don't have the faintest idea. There are plenty of other possible destinations in that direction, but the real question is why she lied."

"Which indicates she didn't want anyone to know where she was going," Rose said, frowning. "I do find this troubling, you know. Faced with the possibility of being tried for murder, one would think she would provide herself with an alibi, even if it were something … embarrassing."

"True. Very true."

"And it would be interesting to know how much later she set out, supposedly for the millinery. Mrs Preston may be able to tell us. If there was a long enough gap, then it isn't likely she followed Mr Holt, stabbed him and returned to her house, is it? He can't have waited long for a hansom, as I believe they are quite plentiful in Beaumont Street."

"They are, and that could be something for me to investigate," Theo said. "I learned the cab driver's name,

William Bellamy, and I hope to have a word with him at some point."

"That's a good idea. He may have remembered something else by now that he didn't tell the police at the time."

"I hope so. Until I speak to Miss Appleby, I tend to feel we are beating our heads against a brick wall, especially in light of your discovery."

There didn't seem to be much else to say on the subject of Irene Appleby and her dubious alibi, so Rose confessed that she had also used the visit to the millinery to order a new hat to wear at the wedding.

"I hope you like it," she said.

"You have excellent taste, I am sure, although I admit that mourning clothes haven't given you much scope to exercise it. I look forward to seeing your new hat, along with whatever dress you will be wearing to be married in." Theo thought for a moment. "Given the temperature in that church, I fully expect you to appear at the altar wrapped in blankets or perhaps a fur coat."

Rose chortled at the vision this presented. "I shall do neither. As it happens, I have a rather sedate gray gown which will be appropriate to wear and should go well with the hat. And a dark blue velvet coat which is warm and just formal enough for a wedding."

"Is it the same dark blue as your beautiful eyes?" Theo smiled at her and Rose felt her cheeks growing warm. One of the ways Theo differed greatly from Edward was the way he often complimented both her looks and her intelligence. It was a refreshing change to know he noticed and admired both aspects. In retrospect, she sometimes felt Edward had more or less taken her for granted and that compliments weren't necessary.

"You'll have to see for yourself," she said. "At least you know I won't be wearing a filmy white dress with a wreath of orange blossoms in my hair." As Theo chuckled, she added,

"I wonder what Miss Appleby looks like? Mrs Preston didn't tell us anything except her age, did she?"

Theo closed his eyes for a moment, as if visualizing a possible Irene Appleby.

"I see her as having fair hair, or light brown, perhaps a bit darker than yours. Blue eyes. Quite small in stature, so as to bring out Mr Holt's protective instincts."

"I don't think protection was quite what he had in mind," Rose objected.

"You know what I mean – he may have thought he was rescuing her from a terrible fate. Let's hope he didn't inadvertently lead her into an even more perilous one. How do you picture her?"

"Tall, slender, with dark hair and brown eyes. A bit exotic, perhaps, with a Spanish or Italian ancestor in her family's past."

"We may both be completely mistaken. Ah well, I shall make her acquaintance tomorrow morning and see what she has to say for herself."

Theo stayed for the evening meal, something he had done on a regular basis since their engagement. It wasn't simply a desire to spend more time in Rose's company, but also a way of avoiding his landlady's cooking. She meant well, but with her extremely limited budget, the meals were often less than appetizing, and Theo was thankful he would not be eating too many more of them.

At the moment he was dividing his time between Rose's house, his rented rooms and Willows, the house they were planning to live in after their wedding. The procedure for buying that house had turned out to be slightly more complicated than anticipated, involving two murders and an unexpected heir to the property title, but they had worked their way through those issues and were now the legal owners.

They had subsequently discovered that Willows needed a good deal of work and redecorating, so Theo had moved his writing desk there and was working on *Honesty for Sale* while supervising the workmen, and only going back to his rented rooms to change his clothes and sleep.

And now there would be another distraction, as he and Rose tried to determine who had stabbed Timothy Holt. Had his attacker intended to kill him or just deliver a warning? Had Holt realized how seriously wounded he was as he started on his journey back to St Clements? Was Irene Appleby responsible, or was someone trying to have her blamed – perhaps hanged – for a crime she hadn't committed?

Normally Theo might have tried to get a few more pages written in the evening, but tonight he found his thoughts were too dominated by Irene Appleby to be able to concentrate. So after he kissed Rose goodbye, he went across St Giles and down a few doors to his rented rooms.

Once inside, he lit a lamp, sat on his bed and considered. If Irene Appleby had not killed Timothy Holt, then who had?

The person most likely to be aggrieved by the affair was Holt's wife. Rose was convinced that she knew about Irene, and she was probably right. Even without first-hand experience of being married, Theo was sure that sort of activity would be suspected, if not proven, by a wife.

Would she go as far as following her husband to his assignation, and then stabbing him as he got into a hansom cab to return home? Possibly. That might depend on whether she had known about Irene for some time, or just discovered her husband's infidelity. Or whether some incident had finally tipped her over the edge.

Another candidate would be a man who wanted Irene for himself and saw Holt as an obstacle. Or maybe Irene herself was the obstacle, if she refused to change her current arrangement. On the other hand, she could have wanted to leave, and Holt had refused to let her go. Theo shook his head, realizing there were too many ways of looking at the matter, and no solid proof of anything.

He shook his head, turned down the lamp and went to bed.

In her own bedroom, Rose was also contemplating Irene Appleby. What sort of background had she come from? Rose would have liked to think Irene was poor, orphaned or both, and so had no alternative but to accept the protection of a wealthy man.

But she was uncomfortably aware that might not be the case. She had heard hushed rumors of women from fairly respectable backgrounds who had similar arrangements. And, she thought wryly, the only difference between those and a marriage entered into for financial benefit was that the marriage was legal, morally sound and more permanent.

She was glad that she couldn't be accused of having taken that route. Although Edward Miles had been wealthy and considered a good match, she had been genuinely fond of him and believed he felt the same about her. Certainly she'd had no reason to think otherwise. Edward's death had ended their marriage after less than two years, but she had assumed it would last for decades and they would grow old together.

But what if it had gone on for years and Edward, possibly bored or seeking diversion, had taken a mistress? How would she have felt? Rose knew she would have been expected to keep quiet, however furious or hurt she might have been. Would she have been angry enough to stab him while he waited to hail a cab after seeing the woman? Or would she have vented her anger on the woman herself?

It was hard to say. She thought for a while, then smiled to herself. At least she knew that sort of decision would never trouble her when she was married to Theo.

Theo rose early the next morning, planning to check on the house repairs and perhaps even write a bit before going to meet Sergeant Bennett at the prison. He debated what would be the most appropriate clothing to wear, thinking that he shouldn't appear too prosperous, to avoid jealousy, but not too scruffy either, which would invite scorn.

He finally settled on his third-best suit, which had been tailored to fit him perfectly but was showing signs of wear, and a hat to match. He took his overcoat and gloves as a concession to the January weather, tucked a clean handkerchief, a pencil and a small notebook into his pocket, and went downstairs for his breakfast.

"Where you off to, then, Mr Stone?" Mrs Rice, his landlady, asked as she set a bowl of steaming porridge and a cup of tea in front of him. "Goin' to see that lady friend of yours?"

"Later, perhaps," Theo said. He eyed the porridge warily, but he felt he couldn't present himself at Rose's breakfast table too often. "I'm actually off to prison first."

As he had predicted, that made Mrs Rice's eyes open wide and she looked out of the window, as if expecting to see police officers surrounding the building. "Are you in trouble again, Mr Stone?"

"Not at all. I'm hoping to get someone *out* of trouble."

"Thank the Lord for that."

Theo wasn't sure which statement that applied to, so he simply dug his spoon into the porridge, trying not to cringe as he ate it. When he had managed to down enough to hold him for an hour or two, he drank a second cup of tea, thanked Mrs Rice for the meal and set off.

Shortly before ten o'clock, Theo walked down Queen Street in the direction of the prison, whose tower he could see long before he arrived. The gray stone walls were forbidding enough from the outside, and he imagined that even though it had recently been extended and modernized, the interior would be equally grim.

Sergeant Bennett was waiting outside the main entrance in New Road, his breath making little clouds in the cold air. He nodded to Theo as he came up.

"Mornin', Mr Stone. Inspector says you're hopin' to get some answers out of that Miss Appleby."

"That's right, Sergeant. 'Hoping' is the correct term."

"Mebbe you'll have more luck than we did. How'd you get mixed up in this, then, if I may ask?"

Theo saw no point in evading the truth. "Do you remember the Preston case?"

"That bailiff what was found dead in the canal?"

"That's the one. After the trial, John Preston's widow subsequently went into service with Irene Appleby. She has been there for the past six months. She holds a fairly high opinion of her employer, and believes she is being held for a crime she did not commit. She asked us to help clear Miss Appleby's name, and we are willing to try."

Bennett drew his eyebrows together, frowning. He had met Mrs Preston. "Has she got any proof Miss Appleby didn't kill this Holt fellow what was keepin' her?"

"No, but as I understand it, neither do the police have any proof that she *did* kill him."

"Fair enough, and I don't mind tellin' you, I don't like her bein' locked up like this. But it ain't my place to say so."

Which was more or less what Theo had suspected. "You can say it to me, Sergeant. I'm inclined to agree. You've met the young woman; what is she like?"

Bennett scratched his head and thought for a minute. "She ain't your average jade off the streets; I'll say that much. She's got more … class … than that. If you're askin' if she'd be capable of stabbin' a man to death, I'd have to say I don't know. Maybe she would if she were provoked enough, maybe she wouldn't. But I reckon, Mr Stone, you'd rather make up your own mind. Shall we go inside and you can see her for yourself?"

"Indeed," Theo said. "Lead the way."

SIX

Theo had been correct in thinking the inside of HM Prison Oxford – to give it its new name – would be nearly as austere as the exterior. It might have been recently updated, but walls, ceilings and floors all seemed to be cold and gray, without a shred of color or warmth, and he shivered as he walked along beside Bennett.

A prison official loomed up in front of them, demanding to know their business, but Bennett brushed him aside with a curt, "We're here to see Irene Appleby. Inspector Reed's orders."

The official gave Theo a long stare, which he supposed was justified, since he was clearly not a police officer, but no further objection was raised. Perhaps the man thought he was a concerned relation, although most respectable families would pretend someone like Irene Appleby had nothing to do with them.

Bennett clearly knew where he was going, and they walked down a corridor and through a door into what Theo surmised was the section where women and children were held. He saw faces that were sad, terrified or resigned, and he wished he could simply open the doors and free them all. Most had probably committed minor crimes as a result of hunger or desperation, but the law was merciless.

They turned a corner and Bennett indicated a doorway. "She's in here, Mr Stone. I'll tell her who you are and then you can talk to her on your own."

"Thank you, Sergeant."

"Inspector said you're to have fifteen minutes, but my watch don't always keep time too good."

"How unfortunate."

Theo set his face in what he hoped was an expression of sober concern and stepped aside as Bennett exchanged a few words with a warden. Their voices were low enough that he couldn't catch the entire conversation, but it appeared a minor argument was taking place. Finally Bennett turned back to Theo.

"He's said you can talk to her in there, but other folks'll be listening, so I said the corridor would be better, and I'll watch to make sure she don't try to escape, not that I think she would do."

"Thank you."

The warden went into the room and came back gripping the arm of a young woman. Theo's first thought was that both he and Rose had been wrong in their guesses about her appearance. She was, as Mrs Preston had told them, probably in her late twenties, but her hair was neither fair nor dark. Instead, it was a rich auburn color, and the eyes that surveyed him curiously were almost green. She was extremely attractive, even under adverse conditions, and he thought it was not too surprising that she had caught Timothy Holt's eye.

Mrs Preston had also been right about the unflattering dress, a dull gray one which hung loosely on the curves of her body. Obviously the prison officials didn't want to give female inmates any reason to feel confident or take any pride in their appearance.

But despite this, Theo sensed a certain defiance in her attitude. She was in danger, but she wouldn't give in without a fight.

"Here's the jade," the warden said. He started to let go of her arm, and she jerked it out of his grasp.

"You can go now," Bennett told him. "I'll be responsible for her."

"I was told …"

"You can go now."

Faced with the sergeant's size and uniformed authority, the warden reluctantly moved off down the corridor. Bennett turned to her and said, "Miss Appleby, I'm Sergeant Bennett, Oxford Police. I don't know if you remember me, but I was here before with Inspector Reed."

"I remember."

"This gentleman is Mr Theodore Stone. He's been asked to look into your case, mebbe see if there's something he can do to help."

"Who asked you to do that, Mr Stone?" She sounded genuinely curious and a little skeptical, as if help was the last thing she expected.

"Mrs Preston. I understand she's in service with you."

"Nell Preston? Yes, she is."

"She's very concerned about you, and she knows that I have had some experience in this area. So with your permission, I'd like to ask you some questions and see if we can move forward at all."

He thought at first she was going to reject his offer, but she was intelligent enough to know she was in serious danger if nothing was done. Perhaps she felt, rightly, that she had nothing to lose by speaking to him. Bennett moved a few feet away to create an illusion of privacy and Irene met Theo's gaze squarely.

"Ask your questions, then," she said.

"First, and I want an honest answer. Did you kill Timothy Holt?"

She didn't pretend to be shocked or outraged. She said simply, "No, I did not."

"Do you know who did?"

He thought he detected a very slight pause before she said, "No."

"Do you have any idea of who might have done? You're obviously intelligent, Miss Appleby, and you must have gone over and over that day in your mind."

She shook her head, immune to flattery. "I don't know. Yes, of course I have thought about it. There isn't much else for me to do in here except contemplate my fate."

Theo noted that whatever her background, Irene Appleby must have received education beyond the basics. She was not only intelligent, but articulate as well.

"How long have you known Mr Holt?" he asked.

"Nearly three years."

"Did he have any enemies that you know of?"

"No. He was liked and respected, as far as I know." For the first time, a smile flickered across her face. "You will understand, Mr Stone, there were large parts of his life I was not involved in."

"But he must have spoken of family and friends over the course of three years."

"Yes, on occasion."

"What was his source of income?"

"Property and investments, I believe. I know very few details."

"You say he occasionally spoke of family and friends. The police have told me he was married. Did his wife know of you, of the arrangement he had with you?"

Again, that very slight pause. "I expect so. Wives usually do, don't they, or so I am advised. Not being a wife, I couldn't say."

"So you believe that Mrs Holt knew about the liaison between you and Mr Holt?"

"Yes."

"Meaning that although he may not have had known enemies, *you* probably had at least one. I can't imagine she felt too kindly toward you."

"I've no idea what she felt. I believe there are some marriages where a wife is almost relieved that her husband takes his pleasure elsewhere."

And that, Theo thought, might well be true, and he shouldn't leap to conclusions. He knew nothing about Mrs Holt, but she wouldn't be the first woman to be grateful to avoid experiencing pregnancy and childbirth on a regular basis, the likely outcome of fulfilling her duties as a wife.

"Was that the case here, do you think?"

"I don't know. That would be far too personal a question for me to ask or him to answer."

Then why had she mentioned it, if not to suggest that Mrs Holt might have seen advantages in the arrangement? It seemed to Theo that over the course of three years, the subject might have arisen at some time, but he pressed onward.

"Did Mr and Mrs Holt have children?"

"Yes, five."

"Of what ages, do you know?"

"The oldest is a boy of about fifteen years, I believe. Forgive me, Mr Stone, but what can that have to do with their father's death?"

"I only wondered if they were of an age to be aware of your arrangement with him, or to understand what it entailed. A fifteen-year-old boy might well be."

"Perhaps, but I doubt he would stab his father to death as a result. I think you must look elsewhere."

"Can you suggest such a place for me to look, then?"

"No," Irene said. "I'm afraid I cannot."

"Very well, let us turn to more practical matters. The day Mr Holt died was Wednesday, a fortnight ago. He had come to see you. Did he say anything to indicate the visit was anything but a usual one?"

For the first time, she didn't answer readily. Theo waited patiently.

"Before he left, he said he might not be able to see me for a while," she said. "He didn't give a reason, and it was not my place to demand one."

"But he didn't indicate he intended to end the relationship."

"No, not at all."

"Only a temporary hiatus, perhaps."

He wondered briefly if she knew what the word meant, and thought perhaps he should clarify it, but she needed no help.

"Perhaps. Of course, it doesn't matter now."

"No, but it may give a clue as to why he died. Could someone have been threatening him? Or demanding money to keep quiet about your relationship? And if he refused …"

Up until now, Irene had been answering his questions more or less unemotionally. Now she appeared to be actively considering the possibility of Timothy Holt being pressured to halt his affair with her and dying as a result of his refusal to do so. Her face was more animated, as if she suddenly saw a glimmer of light or hope.

"I suppose it is possible, but who?"

"You would know better than I, Miss Appleby. Tell me about any of his friends, associates, family members that you know of."

"Oh, heavens, I don't know if I can help you, Mr Stone. I understood his parents had passed away, but he had a brother, called Gregory. He lives somewhere up the Banbury Road, I believe. I expect he helped arrange the funeral. Of course, I wasn't told about it and couldn't have attended. I don't exist in his family's eyes. Or at least I *shouldn't* exist."

He voice was not bitter; she was simply stating a fact. But there was hurt in her face and he realized that she would have liked to bid farewell to the man who had been an important part of her life for three years. Possibly a man she had genuinely liked, even loved.

"Is there anyone else I should know about?"

She thought for a moment. "He had a friend who is a solicitor, Bernard Caldwell. He might know more than I do."

Theo jotted the name in his pocket notebook along with Gregory Holt's name. At least it was a starting point, and a solicitor was more likely to be dispassionate about the matter than a brother.

"Thank you, that could be helpful. And your own family? Is there anyone I should speak to?"

"I have no family. I was a foundling, brought up in an orphanage. So no, there is no one for you to speak to."

"You have no idea who your parents were, or whether you may have other relations unaware of your existence?"

"No. So there is no one to condemn my way of life, and no one to miss me after I am hanged for a murder I did not commit."

She sounded more matter of fact than resigned about her possible fate. Theo didn't think Reed would actually charge her without some evidence, but he couldn't risk waiting to find out.

"Mrs Preston is a staunch ally, Miss Appleby. She will put up a fight to save you, and I am certainly willing to help if I can. Sergeant Bennett did not elaborate, but I should tell you I am half of an investigative agency, and we have kept other people from being unjustly punished."

Irene's green eyes widened a little at that. "And who is the other half of your agency?"

"A lady named Mrs Rose Miles. We work together on cases of all sorts."

"I see. No doubt she will condemn me unseen for my way of life."

Theo thought of Rose's pink cheeks as she had heard of Irene's situation. She wouldn't necessarily approve, but neither would she condemn.

"Mrs Miles will not pass judgement. Like myself, she is more concerned that you not be accused of a crime you didn't commit. That is why you must be completely honest with us."

"I apologize."

"There's no need. I only wanted you to be aware I am not just a useless dilettante or do-gooder. I hope to be of real use to you. I want to go back to the day Mr Holt died. On that day, he visited you. He said he might not be able to come again for a while. What happened after that?"

Theo thought he heard Bennett shift his weight slightly, as if to try and overhear what Irene might say. He remembered Reed saying she had not provided the police with an alibi.

"He left the house."

"On foot?"

"Yes. He would walk to Beaumont Street and hail a cab there to take him home, or wherever else he might be going."

"And on that day, did he indicate he might be going anywhere other than his own house?"

"No."

"And it appears he did go to Beaumont Street, since the cab driver says he boarded the vehicle there. Was there an arrangement for that – that is, did he perhaps ask the driver who had brought him to your house to return after a certain length of time?"

Theo had asked the question partly to see if Irene would confirm Mrs Preston's statement that the cab never came all the way to the house.

"I don't know what arrangements he may have made as to time. I do know he always left the cab in Beaumont Street and walked the remainder of the way, and did the same for the return journey. He said it was more discreet."

"Do you think that was more to protect his own reputation, or to protect yours?"

She actually smiled at that. "You heard the warden, Mr Stone. I may not walk the streets at night looking for customers, but I am still a jade, a fallen woman. I have no reputation to protect."

Theo deliberately ignored the bulk of the statement. He said, "The discretion was for his benefit, then."

"I should think so."

"So it is just possible that his death had nothing to do with you at all, and simply happened to occur on a day when he was visiting you."

"I have no idea. Frankly, I don't see how it could be connected with me, but I am such a convenient suspect the police could hardly avoid blaming me. I suppose people must have seen him come to my door and drew the obvious conclusion."

"I suppose they did. A little questioning in the neighborhood would have then led the police to you. Or he may have said something to the driver that helped them identify you. Now, tell me what you did after Mr Holt left your house that day."

"I went out for a while."

"How much later was that?"

"Not long afterwards. Perhaps a quarter of an hour or so."

"And where did you go?"

Theo almost held his breath, wondering if Irene would offer her story about going to the millinery, or admit she hadn't been there. Or as Rose had suggested, perhaps she had started for the millinery but had been side-tracked or prevented from going there.

"I went for a walk," she said.

"On a cold January day?"

"Yes."

"And where did your walk take you?" He gave her the sort of smile Rose tended to describe as charming. "I know ladies like to look in shop windows, perhaps with an eye to acquiring a new gown or hat."

He didn't miss the way she immediately took the cue he had offered. "Yes, I walked along to Little Clarendon Street, to the shops there."

"Did you call in anywhere, or simply look in the windows?"

"I called in to a millinery."

"And did you purchase a hat?"

"I ordered one, yes. I doubt I will ever have the chance to wear it."

Theo sharpened his tone a little. "This was on the afternoon that Mr Holt died? You are certain of that?"

She met his gaze. "I believe, Mr Stone, you are attempting to establish what I think is called an alibi. Is that so?"

"Yes, and I should think you would have told the police this at once. If you were at the millinery in Little Clarendon Street ordering a new hat, you cannot have been in Beaumont Street or the hansom cab itself stabbing Mr Holt to death, an event which must have been happening at roughly the same time."

"No, I couldn't have been."

Theo almost hated to say anything else. From her calm expression, Irene Appleby thought she had convinced him that she had been discussing a stylish hat when he knew she hadn't been. Rose had been sure the milliner was telling the truth about not having seen Irene for several weeks, and she was good at detecting when people were being less than honest.

Aside from anything else, the milliner knew Irene and would have no reason to lie to Rose, someone she thought was merely a customer, who happened to be acquainted with another customer.

"Miss Appleby," he said calmly. "I told you that Mrs Miles and I work together on cases. You told your servants – or at least Mrs Preston understood – that you were going to the millinery after Mr Holt left the house. You have just told me the same. That appears to give you an alibi for the time of his death, so we wondered why you had not told the police about it.

"Because it was such an odd omission, Mrs Miles went to the millinery in Little Clarendon Street yesterday. The proprietor told her you hadn't been there for at least a month. So I will ask again – where did you go that afternoon?"

SEVEN

Irene just stared at him for a minute. She moved her hands restlessly and Theo felt she was holding herself back with an effort from wringing them. Or alternatively, to keep from slapping his face.

"I'm sorry," he said, "but as I told you, we can't help unless you are completely honest with us."

"You tricked me, Mr Stone."

"And you lied to me, Miss Appleby. I think that evens the score, don't you?"

She sighed. "You are more clever than I first thought, so perhaps you really can help me. No, I did not go to the millinery that afternoon. I went to meet with someone, and I shan't tell you who, only to say again that I did not kill Timothy."

She had never used Holt's first name before, and Theo detected a real note of regret and sorrow in her voice. It might have been primarily a business arrangement between them, but he could see she was grieving.

"You swear to that?"

"Yes."

"And you would do so in court, if it comes to that?"

"Yes."

"But you refuse to provide an alibi which might save your life."

She winced at the blunt statement. "I cannot."

"Tell me, in confidence, did it involve another man? Someone who perhaps wanted you to transfer your loyalty to him?"

Her eyes widened and she said promptly, "No, nothing like that."

Behind him, Theo heard Bennett shift his feet and clear his throat quietly, which he took to mean he had already stretched his allotted time past the limit.

"It is a real pity you have chosen to be so secretive," he said, "so I can only conclude you are trying to protect someone. However, it is you who will face trial as a result of your stubbornness. I believe my time is up now, so I will leave you to think on that. Thank you for the help you did provide, and I hope to speak to you again soon. Perhaps you will have changed your mind by then."

She put a hand out, then withdrew it before he could respond. "I am not unappreciative, Mr Stone. If you can clear my name, I shall be very grateful."

"Very well, we shall leave it at that. I will find out when I may be allowed to speak to you again. Good day, Miss Appleby."

She didn't wait for the warden to escort her, but nodded, turned and went back into the room where she was being held. Theo watched her go and then looked at Bennett.

"Are you ready to go, Mr Stone?" the sergeant asked.

"Yes." They walked down the corridor and when they were well out of earshot, Theo said, "How much of that did you hear?"

"Most of it, I reckon. She's right stubborn, ain't she?"

"She is indeed."

"How'd you know she lied about where she'd been? She wouldn't tell us nothing, but you winkled it out of her right smartish."

"I'm afraid I can't take too much credit. She had told the servants where she was going – or supposedly going – that afternoon, and Mrs Preston told Mrs Miles and myself. It seemed a credible alibi, so Mrs Miles went to the millinery to confirm it, but discovered instead that she hadn't called there for a month or more."

Bennett mulled this for a second or two and then said, "Wonder who it was she was meeting that it's so secret."

"That I can't tell you. I wish I could do."

They had reached the entrance by now and Theo was thankful to step outside into the colder but fresher air. He drew in a deep breath, again feeling a wave of sympathy for the prison's inmates.

"I've got to report back to the inspector," Bennett said. "Seems she's got an alibi of sorts, since she can't have been doin' Mr Holt to death if she was meeting with someone else at the same time, but unless she says who, that don't get us much further forward."

"You have summarized the problem very neatly," Theo said. "Unfortunately, I have no idea of where to start in identifying the other person. Have you spoken to Mr Holt's brother?"

"We have done, and he's been no help at all. He says he didn't know much about Miss Appleby, only that she existed, and he may or may not be tellin' the truth about that. But he was in Banbury all that day, and we found witnesses to prove it. Not that he'd have any reason to kill his brother anyway that we know of."

Theo thought of his own three brothers. However much they had infuriated him on occasion, he could never have done any of them serious harm, and from what he had learned of Timothy Holt, it seemed unlikely he had angered his brother to the point of murder.

"So we must look elsewhere." He smiled ruefully. "Both the police and the Milestone Agency, it would appear. Tell me, Sergeant, which would you say Inspector Reed would prefer – to uncover evidence to convict Miss Appleby of murder or evidence to clear her name?"

"That ain't quite fair, Mr Stone," Bennett said reproachfully. "He don't want to send someone to the gallows or even to trial if they didn't kill anybody. I'd say he just wants to find out who did stab this Mr Holt to death, no matter who it turns out to be."

"I was hoping you'd say that," Theo said. "Very well, we will all try to learn more about what happened that afternoon and see which way the evidence points. If Mrs Miles and I uncover anything new, we will relay it to the police, and vice versa, I should hope."

"I can't speak for the inspector, but I'll see what I can do."

"That's all we can hope for. Thank you for your assistance, Sergeant."

They parted at Carfax, Bennett to go back to the police station in St Aldates, and Theo to walk back up Cornmarket toward Rose's house, turning Irene Appleby's conversation over in his mind.

Rose had her hands full at the time, figuratively speaking, because her mother had chosen that morning to come by and remind her again of her obligations. Charlotte Winters was sitting on the most upright of Rose's armchairs, her elegant skirts spread around her, and was daintily sipping a cup of tea, which she now put down to address her daughter.

"When it comes time to plan your wedding, Rose, remember that it should be discreet and unostentatious. Only the immediate families and perhaps a few close friends. A small wedding breakfast to follow, or you may choose to dispense with that altogether. Summer would be best, I think, or possibly autumn."

"Thank you, Mama, but we are to be married the third week of February. The banns will be read beginning this Sunday. I admit we haven't planned the wedding breakfast yet, but rest assured it will be tasteful. Invitations will be sent out shortly."

That was pure bluff, since she hadn't ordered them yet, but she was sure Mr Nichols, who printed business cards and stationery for the Milestone Agency, wouldn't mind a hurried order. After all, as Charlotte had said, there wouldn't be many guests to invite and not many invitations needed.

"*February?* No, that simply won't do. That will be barely a year since Edward's death."

"That's right. I am extremely lucky, don't you think, to have found someone so quickly whom I love and want to marry?"

Had Charlotte been drinking her tea just then, Rose felt sure she would have choked. As it was, she saw her mother's fingers tighten on the cup handle and hoped she wouldn't throw it.

"That is a remark in very poor taste, Rose, and hardly respectful to Edward."

"Is it? I can't see that it has anything to do with Edward, and I am sure he would not have wanted me to spend the rest of my life alone. Theo and I are very compatible, and I am certain we will be happy together."

From Charlotte's expression, it seemed that happiness ranked fairly low on the list of desirable qualities in a marriage. But she may have reflected that at least Rose would be safely married, and not a well-to-do young widow who might be preyed upon by unscrupulous men.

Until very recently, Charlotte had placed Theo in that category, and it had been something of a unpleasant surprise when she learned how much income his novels were generating. Charlotte loathed the means, but reluctantly accepted the results.

She cast around for a safer subject. "I understand you are refurnishing the house Mr Stone has purchased. Is it going well?"

Rose noted that Theo was still going to be referred to by his surname for a while and also that her mother didn't think she had contributed anything toward the house purchase price, which wasn't true.

"Quite well, I believe. Theo has been spending a great deal of time there, supervising the workmen. My role has been mostly to choose items such as carpet, tiles and wallpaper."

Charlotte was obviously relieved that Rose wouldn't be found up a ladder or with a hammer or paintbrush in her hand.

"I am sure your taste is excellent. And is that where he is at the moment?"

"No," Rose said. She glanced at the clock on the mantelpiece, which showed a quarter past ten. "I expect he is in Oxford Prison."

By the time Theo reached her house, Rose had explained to her mother that he was a visitor at the prison and not an inmate. That did not noticeably reassure Charlotte, who had never liked the idea that her daughter was involved in an investigative agency.

So Rose didn't bother to tell her that she had been attempting to confirm the alibi of a woman suspected of murdering the man who had been keeping her as his mistress. It was just possible that the Holts were known to Charlotte, but unlikely that she would want to contribute anything she knew about them to the investigation. Without even asking, Rose knew Charlotte's view would be that Irene Appleby deserved anything coming to her, whether or not she was guilty.

So she provided her mother with a second cup of tea, listened to some gossip about people she wasn't interested in, and finally saw her into her carriage for the short ride back to the family home. She sighed in relief as the carriage moved off. Rose knew that her mother, for all her criticism, had her daughter's best interests at heart, and didn't want either her or the family's reputation to suffer. It was just annoying that Charlotte didn't seem to trust anyone's judgement but her own.

She had time to attend to a few household chores before Theo arrived, and from his expression, she knew his conversation with Irene Appleby had not been entirely successful. They settled in the drawing room, where Theo was provided with a cup of hot tea.

"That is most welcome," he said, wrapping his hands around the cup. "I do wish people would commit murders in more clement weather. Still, we are sitting by the fireside, which is a great improvement on the interior of the prison."

"Is it truly horrible?"

"I think 'grim' is the best word to describe it. Anyway, I was able to speak to Miss Appleby, and to start at the end of our conversation, you were quite correct about her not going to the millinery on the afternoon in question."

"She admitted that?" Rose was surprised that Irene had abandoned her supposed alibi, even when it had been proven false.

"Yes. Unfortunately, she won't say where she did go. She says only that she going to meet with someone, but refuses to say who that was, except that it was *not* a man trying to woo her away from Timothy Holt."

"I wonder why she won't say. Is she trying to protect someone?"

"That was my first thought, too. I don't know who it might be."

Rose leaned forward in her chair. "Tell me about her, Theo, and everything she said to you. It's just possible I may pick up something you didn't think important."

"Something a mere man would have missed?" Theo grinned at her. "Very well, I shall do my best."

He started with a physical description, noting that they had both pictured her incorrectly.

"It's possible she has some Scottish or Irish blood, with that auburn hair and green eyes. It's very striking, and she is certainly attractive, although she was obviously not at her best after a week in prison. She says she was a foundling, raised in an orphanage, so claims not to know anything of her own family background."

"Did you believe her?"

"I suppose so. The only reason she would have to lie about that is if her family has disowned her, or something of that sort."

"You would think if there were any relations in Oxford, they would have come to her aid, regardless of her affair with Mr Holt. After all, she has not been charged with a crime. Go on, Theo."

He described the way Irene had jerked her arm away from the warden and then went on to relate the remainder of the conversation.

"Did she seem distressed that we had found she lied about where she was that afternoon?" Rose asked, when he had finished.

"I wouldn't say exactly distressed. More … exasperated. And a bit irritated, I think, that we had already proved ourselves to be one step ahead of her."

"And one step ahead of the police, who surely would have found out at some point."

"Yes. On the other hand, the police have taken one step we have not, since we didn't know about him. Timothy Holt had a brother, Gregory, and Sergeant Bennett tells me they have confirmed he was in Banbury that day, so he is neither the murderer nor the person Miss Appleby was meeting."

"He could have hired someone else to do the deed, you know. But is there any motive at all for him to want his brother dead?"

"Not that the police have discovered," Theo said. "It seems a bit far-fetched to think Gregory killed him out of disapproval for his keeping a mistress, and it sounds as if the family as a whole was well off enough that money isn't likely to have been an issue."

"He may have coveted Miss Appleby, though. You said she is very attractive."

"I suppose that is possible, but there are drawbacks to that theory."

Rose nodded and reached for the teapot to refill the cups. "Yes, I can see at least two. Firstly, that he was not physically present in Oxford, and secondly, that if he desired her, he would hardly place her in such a perilous position."

"You wouldn't think so. Unless he intends to appear at the last minute as a knight on a white horse to reveal the identity of the true assassin and rescue her from the gallows."

Rose burst out laughing. "That scenario is what I would expect from the author of sensational novels," she said. "However, conspiring in his brother's death seems a extreme method of securing her affection. Besides, if she was fond of Mr Holt, she would hardly be endeared to anyone connected to his death. She would learn the truth at some point."

"You are practical, as always." Theo drank his tea. "I can't help feeling, though, that Gregory Holt might have something to contribute. He may well know things about his brother that neither of the women in Timothy's life knew. I think I will try and see him."

"And the solicitor as well?"

"Yes, although in my experience, solicitors are exasperatingly close-mouthed about their clients. With luck, he will have been a personal friend as well as a professional associate. Miss Appleby seemed to think he was. I think the first person to speak to, however, is William Bellamy, the cab driver."

"He may be difficult to locate, don't you think? There are a great many cab drivers in Oxford, and I don't imagine they always follow a set route. And aside from that, when you do find him, he will probably say he has already spent quite enough time talking about Mr Holt when he was interviewed by the police."

"You are correct, and that is why we are going to be working as a team on this."

Rose's eyes sparkled as she contemplated doing something more interesting than quizzing a milliner about her customer.

"What did you have in mind, Theo?"

"Well, I will first find Bellamy, and when I have identified him, you could be a bereaved relative of the late Timothy Holt. A fairly distant relative would be best, and of course you won't provide your name. Not your real name, anyway. You will insist that the cab driver must have seen something to give a clue as to his assassin – that's a good word to use, by the way – and that he must tell you what it is so that justice can be done. Do you think you can do that?"

"I'll do my best," Rose said.

EIGHT

"I'm sure you will perform admirably," Theo said. "I was thinking I might visit my parents first, and see if either of them know anything about the Holt family as a whole. Since Timothy Holt lived somewhere near St Clements, their paths may have crossed. I expect William Bellamy will keep for a while."

"That's a good idea," Rose said. "I considered asking my mother when she called earlier, but I knew that even if she were acquainted with Mrs Holt, they would hardly have discussed Mr Holt's mistress. I don't imagine either of them would even acknowledge Irene Appleby's existence. Your mother seems a bit more broad-minded and less judgemental."

"Or more realistic, at any rate. She would hardly give the relationship her whole-hearted approval, but she would understand why a young woman with no assets other than her looks and personality might accept an offer such as the one Mr Holt made to her."

Rose was quiet, thinking of the decisions Irene would have had to make, knowing that any respectability she had would be sacrificed in order to have a roof over her head and food on the table. What would she herself have done in similar circumstances? Rose couldn't even imagine, having always had all she needed provided without question or any effort on her part.

Finally she said, "I think that is rather magnanimous of your mother. Those of us who have never had to struggle would find it hard to understand, but at least I recognize how fortunate I have been."

"And will continue to be, I hope," Theo said, smiling. "I shall call on my father at the brewery, to see if he has ever crossed paths with Timothy or Gregory Holt, and then after lunch I shall call on my mother."

"And what shall I do, besides provide you with a meal in between your errands?" Rose was aware she sounded a bit snappish, but Theo didn't seem to mind.

"Well, I understand you have a wedding to plan, so perhaps you would want to get on with that? I am sure there is more to be done than ordering your new hat, but I don't pretend to know what it might be."

"Yes, I did tell my mother invitations would be sent shortly, so I suppose I should order them from Mr Nichols. I'm sorry, Theo, I didn't mean to sound churlish; I know we have always agreed you would do most of the physical side of our investigations."

"Your contributions are just as valuable, as you know, and Sergeant Bennett was most impressed at your debunking of Miss Appleby's alibi. If you are willing to wait until I have been to the brewery and we have had lunch, we could ride together as far as the High Street for you to visit the print shop."

"I suppose it would be too much to hope for that William Bellamy would be driving the cab we hailed," Rose said. "Yes, that sounds a good plan."

While Theo set off for his family's brewery, Rose sat down to decide what the wedding invitations should say. There was an accepted form of wording, she knew, although she had never had to compose an invitation to a small second wedding, or to any wedding, for that matter. Before her marriage to Edward, her mother had taken charge of the arrangements, leaving Rose with little to do but dress and have her hair done before the ceremony. She dipped her pen in the inkwell and wrote:

Mr Theodore Thomas Stone and Mrs Rose Elizabeth Miles
request the honour of your presence at their wedding
Twelve O'Clock, 18th February, Eighteen Hundred and
Eighty-two
Holy Trinity Church, Walton Street, Oxford
Wedding Breakfast to follow at 21 St Giles Street

It would have been preferable, she thought, to have the reception at Willows, but there was no guarantee all the work on the house would be finished in time, and Rose didn't want their guests being greeted by half-papered rooms or the smell of fresh paint. Besides, her cook would be more comfortable preparing the food in a kitchen she was familiar with, and one guaranteed to be fully functional on the day.

She saw no need to add an RSVP to the invitations, either, considering the small number of guests to be invited. If there was any food left over, she was sure Theo's three younger brothers would make short work of it.

Satisfied with the invitation's wording, she put the paper aside to show to Theo before taking it to the printer.

Theo went through the gates of the brewery, sniffing the familiar odor of hops and yeast that permeated the air around it. His family's brewery was one of several in the area, and Theo sometimes wondered if the workers who lived nearby were so used to the smell that they no longer noticed it, or if they simply regarded it as the source of their income.

He made his way to his father's office and tapped on the door.

"Come in."

Theo opened the door and entered. He was more assured of a welcome these days than he had been as a struggling writer, when his father had been expecting a plea for funds whenever his eldest son appeared. Thomas Stone might not understand why Theo had chosen this way of life, but he recognized sound business practice when he saw it.

"Good morning, Theodore. What brings you here?"

"Good morning, Father. I'm really just in search of information."

"Do sit down. What is it – background for a book?"

"Only very indirectly. It may become one in future." Theo pulled a straight-backed chair up and sat on it. "I know you are busy, so I shall go straight to the point. Have you ever made the acquaintance of either of these two brothers – Timothy or Gregory Holt? "

Thomas frowned at him. "Timothy Holt? Wasn't that the man who was found dead in a hansom cab a fortnight or so ago?"

"That's right. I suppose you read about it in the *Journal*."

"Yes, I did. What have you to do with him?"

"We are looking into the matter on behalf of someone whom the police suspect of possible involvement in his death."

"That is a very mealy-mouthed explanation," Thomas said sternly. "Have the police made an arrest, then?"

Theo sighed. "A young woman who was Holt's mistress is being held in Oxford Prison. She has not been formally charged with anything as yet, and she completely denies having anything to do with his murder. We – Rose and I – tend to believe her."

"You do become involved in some rather unsavory matters," Thomas said. He was merely stating a fact rather than a criticism, and Theo took it as such. "But to answer your original question; I have never actually met either of the Holt brothers, although I have heard of them."

"In what context, may I ask?"

"The family has a considerable income from property, I believe, and both the brothers are known to be investors in various business ventures. They don't run the businesses themselves, but simply provide operating funds, especially for businesses just being started. I know no particulars except that their investments are widespread, so if one company they have backed experiences difficulties, another may compensate."

"Their financial eggs aren't all in one basket, you mean."

"Exactly."

"Did they work together, do you know? That is to say, if Timothy promised funds to someone, would Gregory have to be informed and approve of that?"

"I don't know for certain," Thomas said. "I believe, however, they operated independently, although they may well have discussed their actions with each other."

"I don't suppose you know of anyone who would like to see them fail completely? To the extent of eliminating one of them?"

"No, I don't. As I said, I know no particulars of their investments. And there are more subtle ways of ruining a man in Holt's position than knifing him to death in a cab. Far too melodramatic, I would say."

"But effective," Theo said. "And so far, Timothy Holt's killer has escaped detection."

"Unless you and Rose are mistaken in your evaluation of his mistress's innocence."

"I don't think we are, to be honest. I have spoken to her and received an impression of intelligence, as well as a certain affection for Holt which extended beyond his generosity in paying her bills. The problem is that although she insists she did not kill him, she refuses to say where she was at the time, only that she was meeting with someone. She won't say who that was."

"Then it sounds as if you are in something of a cul-de-sac. I am sorry I can't help you any further, Theodore, but all I know of either of the Holt brothers was that they were quite astute in their investments."

He looked at Theo over the top of his spectacles and a smile twitched the corners of his mouth. "That might include Timothy Holt's investment – if we may call it such – in the young woman."

Theo considered that, coupled with his father's previous comment about someone possibly wanting to ruin them financially.

"I wonder if someone was jealous of their success? I have to admit that with his mistress in the picture, the only jealousy we were considering was something involving her, for example, if another man coveted her and made her a better offer. Having seen her, I can understand how that might happen. But a business rival could also be jealous, possibly enough to kill in the heat of the moment."

"And was such a rival seen in the vicinity?" Thomas asked. "From what I read in the *Journal*, the attack must have been made more or less publicly, but must also have been premeditated. Generally speaking, businessmen do not carry lethal knives with them to employ in the heat of the moment – as you describe it – if someone angers them. I suppose an assassin could be hired, but again, he would have been seen."

"Like Rose, you are always practical," Theo said, grinning. "You are quite right, of course. The cab driver says he saw no one near, but Timothy Holt was not stabbed by an invisible hand. Someone was there, armed with a knife, and was close enough to drive a blade into him without drawing attention to themselves."

"So the cab driver either was not looking in the right direction, was temporarily distracted, or is lying. And the attack was planned in advance by someone who obviously intended to evade notice."

"Yes," Theo said. "I'm afraid that sums it up. Thank you for your information, Father, which at least gives me something else to consider. Apparently Holt lived somewhere in the vicinity of St Clements, so after lunch, I am going to call on mother and see if she knows the Holts socially."

He stood up and shook hands with his father, reflecting that Thomas was a hard-headed businessman who wouldn't have hesitated to share any facts he knew about the Holt brothers, but who wouldn't repeat mere gossip. That was commendable, but not necessarily helpful.

"If anything should happen to come your way," he said, "any scrap of information you feel might be useful, will you let me know?"

"Yes, of course. Like you, I would not want to see anyone hanged for a murder they did not commit."

It was one of the few times his father had acknowledged that the Milestone Agency might be more than a harmless hobby, which pleased Theo, and he walked back to Rose's house, turning over the information he had received.

Timothy Holt had invested money in various businesses, ones that he felt would return a profit. His brother had apparently done the same. It would perhaps be helpful to know which businesses they had backed, but Theo's heart sank at the idea of trying to track them down. Besides, he had a feeling the motive behind Holt's death was a far more personal one, and that even if she hadn't wielded the knife, Irene Appleby was somehow involved.

Rose took out the wedding invitation and displayed it to him. "What do you think? I believe it covers all the essential points."

"I agree. That will do admirably."

"So I will take it to Mr Nichols at the print shop and ask him to print … thirty, do you think? We shouldn't need too many."

"That should be enough. I have numerous relations whom it will be a positive pleasure to exclude."

Rose eyed him uneasily. She had met his parents and his brothers, but was largely unaware of anyone else in his larger circle of relations.

"If there's anyone you feel you should invite, of course you should do so. After all, even though we have agreed to have a small wedding, we are both being married, not just me."

Theo chuckled. "I know that, my dear. It's nothing to do with you, the fact that you have been married before, or the scope of the wedding. It's just that between their hectoring me to marry a brewery heiress and their dislike of my writing career – even though I strongly suspect they have bought and read the books – I prefer to present them with a *fait accompli* rather than invite them to the scene of the crime, as it were."

"Oh, I see," Rose said, relieved. "I'll order thirty, then. Shall we have something to eat now and you can tell me whether your father was able to supply any additional information about the Holt brothers?"

"An excellent idea."

Over lunch, Theo told her the little that Thomas Stone knew about Timothy and Gregory Holt.

"Apparently they supply what I believe is called seed money to get new businesses started, in return for a percentage of the profits once they are up and running. I suppose that is slightly risky, but I expect they have been doing it long enough to be fairly astute judges of the likelihood of a business succeeding or not."

"And what happens if the business is not successful?" Rose asked.

"I imagine they lose money on the venture. Why, are you thinking some unsuccessful entrepreneur took out his frustration on Timothy Holt by stabbing him?"

"It could happen, I imagine. But identifying such a person would be quite difficult. From what your father said, the two brothers didn't necessarily work together, so Gregory might not have known what Timothy was investing in."

"No, so if Timothy made a bad investment, it would only affect him. I wonder if that is what happened and was the reason he told Miss Appleby he couldn't see her for a while."

"Or conversely," Rose said, "he was going to be so involved in some new venture that he wouldn't have the opportunity to call on her."

"Or the funds to do so."

They halted their conversation while Cora cleared the table, and then Rose said, "Will you be able to speak to her again?"

"I hope so. I shall ask Inspector Reed if it will be possible. However, from what she told me, Mr Holt did not discuss business matters with her. She only knew that he had income from property and investments, which is precisely what my father also said."

"Well, women are not thought to be able to understand financial matters."

"What nonsense. I suspect that given the opportunity, my mother could manage the brewery as efficiently as my father, not that I would tell either of them that."

"No, that would hardly be prudent."

"You don't suppose ..." Theo stopped.

"What?"

"That Miss Appleby had any ideas of starting up a business of her own? After all, she can't have expected their arrangement to last forever, and he was in an ideal position to bankroll her. She struck me as quite intelligent and capable of running … oh, I don't know … a dress shop, perhaps. Or something similar. It would have to be something she had knowledge of."

"I trust you don't mean a brothel."

Theo gulped and wondered how much Rose knew about such establishments. "No, I didn't. A far more respectable enterprise."

"It's possible. You could ask her when you speak to her again."

"I think I will. Shall we find a cab and call on Mr Nichols?"

The hansom cab rattled through Cornmarket and turned into the High Street. Theo had chatted briefly with the driver before they set off, long enough to establish that he wasn't William Bellamy, but that he had heard of his misfortune and was appalled on his behalf.

"Can't trust nobody," he said. "Weren't Will's fault if somebody took it into their heads to stab his passenger, but the way the coppers went after him, you'd think it was."

"I'm sure he wasn't to blame," Theo said, hoping that was true. After all, Bellamy would have had the best chance of anyone to drive a knife into Holt without being noticed, but as far as anyone knew, he totally lacked a reason to do so. He was also pleased to hear the police had done a thorough job of questioning Bellamy. It indicated they might not be quite as eager to accuse Irene Appleby as it had first seemed.

"Course he weren't to blame," the driver said. "Fellow couldn't pay Will if he were dead, could he?"

Faced with that impeccable logic, Theo could only agree, and had joined Rose inside the cab for the journey. They were nearly to the print shop when the driver halted the cab, and Theo put his head out of the window to see why. It was always a busy part of the street, but seemed to be even busier than usual today, and as he craned his neck, he could see that the obstruction wasn't a normal one.

Vehicles had been stopped from going through, and several uniformed police officers were in the street, trying vainly to keep curious onlookers away from whatever was happening. Theo thumped on the cab roof.

"We'll get out here. We're only going a bit further."

He helped Rose out and paid the driver. They approached the center of the activity and Theo saw Sergeant Bennett among the officers. With Rose holding his arm, he maneuvered his way through the onlookers until he could see that the officers and Dr Cutler, the police surgeon, were gathered around a huddled figure in the street. Theo waved his free arm and caught Bennett's eye. The sergeant came over to where Theo could speak to him without shouting.

"What's happened, Sergeant?" he asked.

"Man's been stabbed to death."

"Who is he, do you know?"

"Oh, we know all right," Bennett said grimly. "Other cab driver told us who he was."

"Cab driver?" Rose asked, while a cold shiver ran down Theo's spine.

"That's right, ma'am." Bennett nodded toward the figure on the ground, whom they could just glimpse through the forest of legs and skirts. "William Bellamy, driver of the cab when Mr Holt was done to death."

NINE

"And I suppose," Theo said to Bennett, "that once again, no one saw anything helpful."

"That's right. Too busy screamin' their heads off to pay attention to anything else."

"How unfortunate," Rose said. "But I would say that one fact about Mr Bellamy's death is very clear."

"What's that, ma'am?" Bennett looked as though he would welcome any fact, clear or not.

"His death and Mr Holt's are almost certainly connected. First the passenger, then the driver, both killed in the same manner. I would go so far as to say both murders were probably committed by the same person. And since she is still in prison, that person defnitely was not Irene Appleby."

Bennett looked as though she had just informed him that two plus two equaled four. Theo supposed in the hurry to get to the crime scene and try to ascertain what had happened, that thought had not yet occurred to him.

"No, it couldn't be her," he said.

"So I hope Inspector Reed will arrange for her immediate release and concentrate on connecting and solving the two crimes. We shan't keep you any longer, Sergeant, as I know you have much to do."

Bennett drew himself up and stopped just short of saluting Rose, who smiled warmly. He turned and walked away and Theo said, "Well reasoned. The police would have realized sooner or later that Miss Appleby could not have committed this crime, but perhaps you have saved them some time."

"So you agree the same person was responsible for both deaths?"

"Oh, yes, I agree. Hopefully Inspector Reed will, too. It is just too much of a coincidence that once both we and the police started looking into Timothy Holt's death more closely, the person who was most likely to hold information about it is killed in exactly the same manner."

Rose chuckled and Theo said, "You find that amusing?"

"No, not at all. I was only thinking that I shall never find out how convincing I would have been as a grieving relation of Mr Holt's, trying to pry information from Mr Bellamy."

"I'm sure you would have played your part to perfection, but it may be just as well you didn't have the chance, not with a knife-wielding assassin about. Especially one who seems to be able to vanish without leaving a trace. Look, there's Inspector Reed."

Reed had come striding down the High Street, probably having been summoned from his office at the police station. He gave Theo and Rose no more than a brief curious glance as he passed, but they both knew he would be speaking to them at some point to see if they could provide any information, or alternatively, demanding to know why they happened to be present at the scene of a murder.

The crowd of onlookers began to drift away, sensing that nothing else interesting was going to happen and that they might be called as witnesses if they loitered too long. It was one thing to observe the aftermath of a crime, but quite another to have to appear in court to describe what they'd seen.

Reed and Dr Cutler were conversing earnestly and Theo would have given a great deal to eavesdrop. He supposed they would have to wait and see what details, if any, the inspector was willing to share with them.

"I don't imagine he'll want to speak to us just now," Rose said, echoing his thoughts. "Shall we carry on and order the invitations?"

"We may as well. I was going to leave you to attend to it, but I admit to feeling a little uneasy about that now."

"Besides, you are acquainted with Mr Nichols and I am not. So shall we go together?"

They walked the short distance to the print shop, and Theo introduced Rose to the printer, failing to keep a somewhat smug look off his face when he saw the impression she was making on Mr Nichols. Rose produced her rough draft of the wedding invitation and also ordered some calling cards with *Mrs Rose E. Stone* to be engraved on them. Mr Nichols, slightly flustered and obviously eager to please, promised the order would be completed by the end of the week.

"I did feel rather self-conscious," Rose admitted to Theo when they had left the shop. "Such a pleasant man, isn't he?"

"He was totally besotted by you," Theo said. "Understandably, of course. I see I shall have to beat other men off on a regular basis. A mere husband won't stand a chance."

"Oh, Theo, what nonsense." She took his arm again and looked down the High Street. "It looks as though they are taking Mr Bellamy away now."

"And a few ghouls are still watching, although I can't imagine what they expect to see. They certainly won't see anyone led away in handcuffs, since this killer appears to be just as invisible as Mr Holt's was. Or perhaps we should say, they have managed to be as invisible this time as they were before."

"I confess," Rose said, "that I did wonder at first whether Mr Bellamy was responsible for Mr Holt's death. After all, he could easily have reached into the interior of the cab on some pretext and stabbed him. At those close quarters, and taken by surprise, it would have been almost impossible for Mr Holt to defend himself."

"Yes, I agree he could have done, and even though we know of no motive, he could have been paid to commit the crime. But assuredly he did not stab himself to death in the middle of the High, so whether he killed Mr Holt or not, the motive here is far more obvious."

"Yes. To stop him from talking, so that any information he possessed has died with him."

They watched as Bellamy's body was loaded onto a stretcher and then placed inside a vehicle Theo tentatively identified as a mortuary van. It turned around and rolled up the street, passing them, as the few people still hovering at the scene were shooed away by Sergeant Bennett and another constable.

"We can say he was killed to stop him from talking," Theo said, "but I wonder if Mr Bellamy had already discussed his unsettling experience with anyone else. Mr Holt was killed a fortnight ago – that would have given him plenty of time to have chatted with other cab drivers, friends in a pub, his wife if he had one ..."

"Quite possibly. It must have been very upsetting, so it would be odd if he hadn't mentioned it to someone. You remember our driver just now knew he had been questioned by the police."

"Yes, and I doubt he was an isolated case."

"So that must be worrying Mr Holt's attacker. Locating whoever he spoke to, however, will not be easy. Except, perhaps for his wife, assuming he was married. If he was, Inspector Reed or someone will no doubt be speaking to her soon, to tell her of his death."

They exchanged speculative looks and Theo said, "No, I don't think we should dog his footsteps, hoping to get a word with Mrs Bellamy. After all, we were hired – or at least asked

– to clear Irene Appleby's name, and now it would appear that has been accomplished, although admittedly not by us."

"True. But neither we nor the police are any closer to knowing who stabbed Timothy Holt. So perhaps we should go on and speak to your mother and see what she knows of him. Or at least you should."

"I think," Theo said firmly, "We should stay together for a while. And I admit to feeling rather uneasy about hailing a cab. I know it's cold, but would you mind a brisk walk to Iffley Road?"

The route to Iffley Road inevitably took them past the place where William Bellamy had breathed his last, and just as inevitably, Inspector Reed stepped into their path and said politely, "Good afternoon. Could I just have a brief word with you both?"

"Certainly, Inspector," Theo said. "It may save time if we tell you we already know some of what happened here. Sergeant Bennett told us William Bellamy was stabbed to death. Obviously this happened only a short time ago, and it would appear the attacker was not identified, since you have not apprehended anyone."

Reed was momentarily lost for words, but recovered quickly. "No, we do not know who was responsible. The High is always crowded with vehicles and pedestrians, and it would be extremely easy for someone to disappear after the attack without attracting notice. I assume from your comment that you and Mrs Miles did not see anything that might help?"

"I'm afraid not," Rose said. "We only arrived at the point where a crowd had already gathered."

"May I ask how you happened to be here?"

"We were on our way to the print shop near the top of the street to order our wedding invitations." She gave Reed a rather shy smile, which Theo felt was manufactured for the occasion. It wouldn't work; Reed was too aware of Rose's intelligence to be taken in by artificial feminine wiles.

"And then, having observed the commotion further down the street, you felt obliged to investigate."

"As would most people," Theo said. "We spoke briefly to Sergeant Bennett and then having established the basic facts, we went back to the print shop. We are now on our way to see my mother in Iffley Road, a route which sadly takes us past this point."

"Walking, rather than hailing a cab?"

"I believe," Theo said, "we have rather lost the taste for cab travel. Is it possible for you to share any details at all concerning Mr Bellamy's death?"

"There are very few details to share, Mr Stone, but I see no harm in sharing them with you." Reed took out a small notebook and consulted it. "It appears William Bellamy had driven down Queen Street to the top of the High, just past Carfax. He stopped there to let his passenger off."

"Who was the passenger?"

"We have not located him – or her – and perhaps never will, but Bellamy was alive and well at that point. He was seen by several witnesses to be inspecting the harness whilst waiting for someone else to require his services. As you know, there are often people offering items for sale at Carfax, and he spoke briefly to two or three of them. They noticed nothing amiss."

"So when did …"

"He was then approached by a man called John Meredith who asked to be driven to Headington. That is a long drive and Mr Meredith says Bellamy was perfectly willing to undertake it, perhaps thinking of the substantial fare involved. Mr Meredith got into the cab and a minute later, they started off. Progress is always a bit slow in the High, but then here, only a hundred yards or so further, the cab stopped completely for no obvious reason. Mr Meredith, understandably puzzled, thumped on the roof to get Bellamy's attention, and the response was a series of shouts and screams from passers-by.

"Bellamy had toppled from his seat onto the ground, mortally wounded. Mr Meredith actually saw him fall past the window of the cab. He immediately disembarked, and along with several other people, tried to help staunch the blood flow, but without success. Dr Cutler said that was not surprising, as a sharp blade of some sort had penetrated his chest to a depth of three or four inches."

"Good heavens," Rose said. "And have you exonerated Mr Meredith?"

"As much as possible," Reed said. "He didn't know Bellamy's name, had never seen him before and hailed a cab at random. We will speak to him again, of course, but at this moment there is no reason to think he is guilty of anything but wanting to travel to a distant part of Oxford."

"So Mr Bellamy had to have been attacked near Carfax, before Mr Meredith actually hailed the cab," Rose said. "He saw nothing out of the ordinary? If Mr Bellamy had already been attacked at that point, one would think he would have displayed some indication of it. Surely he must have known, or been in pain."

"Mr Meredith was simply looking for an unoccupied cab," Reed said drily. "The condition of the driver was not of any real interest to him and if Bellamy was in pain, he seemed inclined to ignore it in favor of a large potential fare. There are always people milling about there, and no, Mr Meredith says he noticed nothing out of the ordinary. No one thrusting a knife into Bellamy, or conversely, wiping a bloody blade on their sleeve."

"Or on a handkerchief?" Rose suggested. "That could be discarded far more easily, and I don't imagine a cheap handkerchief with no identifying marks could be traced to its owner."

Reed looked at her curiously. "I do hope you never take to crime, Mrs Miles," he said. "We will, of course, be examining closely both the place where the fatal journey began and the place where Bellamy actually died. I somehow doubt we will find anything in either of them that will definitely identify his killer."

"Well, you know it wasn't Irene Appleby," Theo said, and was rewarded with a critical glance.

"No, it wasn't. That must please you, since you have taken up her cause."

"So will she now be released? It seems next to certain that the two murders are not only connected but probably committed by the same person, don't you think?"

"Possibly."

"Oh, come now, Inspector," Rose said. "You as much as admitted you were holding her because you had no more likely suspect. Now you do, but he – or she, I suppose – is wandering freely about Oxford. Surely you could allow Miss Appleby to go home, with the proviso that she keep herself available for further questioning if necessary."

She smiled at Reed, as if she had stated something so obvious that all he needed to do was nod and agree with her. Theo didn't think the inspector could resist, and so was not surprised when he said, "It may well be possible."

"Good. From what Mr Stone tells me, the prison is not a pleasant place."

"It is not intended to be."

"I was about to add, especially for someone who has not committed a crime."

"I daresay. Once I have learned a bit more about Bellamy's death, I will speak to Miss Appleby again, and if I am convinced she had nothing to do with this second crime, I will arrange for her to be released. With the proviso, as you suggest, that she remain in Oxford and be available for further questioning if needed."

"An excellent plan," Theo said. "If there is nothing more we can contribute, Inspector, we will be on our way and leave you to your work. If you need to speak to us again, you know where you can find us later this afternoon or evening."

"I do indeed. Good day."

"Good day."

They continued their walk down the High Street and eventually came to the junction known as The Plain, where they turned into Iffley Road.

Neither of them had said much as they walked, but now Rose said, "Mrs Preston will be delighted if Miss Appleby is allowed to return to her home, won't she? I can't help wondering, however, what will happen to the household now that Mr Holt can no longer fund it."

"Perhaps she will find another benefactor," Theo said. "Or as we mentioned, she may actually be able to establish a small business enterprise of some sort. I imagine Gregory Holt might be able to arrange some discreet financing."

"If he is so inclined. We know little about him, and he may be more puritanical than his brother."

"With luck, he will not be on close terms with his sister-in-law. If you are correct and Mrs Holt knew about Miss Appleby's relationship with her late husband, she would hardly approve of providing her with any help at all."

"Her approval wouldn't be required," Rose said. "Not only would it be her brother-in-law, rather than her husband, providing the funds, but wives are not as a rule allowed to have any say in financial matters, even if it directly concerns them. It is thought they don't understand anything involving money."

"Despite all the evidence to the contrary," Theo said, smiling.

They stopped in front of a substantial brick house with an immaculate front step and polished brass knocker on the front door. "Well, here we are. I hope my mother does not have a flock of callers, or if she does, that they are all madly gossiping about the late Timothy Holt and his mistress. Let's find out."

TEN

Theo lifted the brass knocker and rapped on the door. It took a few minutes before it was answered, which he hoped meant that his mother was busy with gossipy callers and the housemaid had been drafted in to serve tea and cakes. The Stones weren't quite grand enough to have a butler, something that always amused Theo. Pickett would have sneered – discreetly – if he had known.

Hetty opened the door to them, her face lighting up when she saw Rose had accompanied him.

"Do come in, Mr Theodore, and …" She hesitated, unsure of the proper form of address.

"Mrs Miles," Theo said, "but not for much longer, as you probably have been told."

"Oh, yes, sir."

"Does my mother have callers, Hetty?"

"Only Mrs Minton. I know she'll be pleased you have called."

Rose felt slightly guilty that their call was less a social one and more a means of gathering information, but at least she had met Mrs Minton before, and knew her to be a friendly neighbor. More importantly, she was a chatty source of local gossip, which could be useful.

Theo had much the same reaction, and said easily, "I haven't spoken to Mrs Minton in some time. It will be a pleasure to renew the acquaintance."

"Yes, sir."

Hetty took their coats and saw them into the drawing room, where a coal fire was providing welcome warmth. Theo's mother, Katherine, and her caller were seated in armchairs near it, with a low table between them holding the tea tray.

"Theodore, how lovely to see you," Katherine said. "And you've brought Rose as well. Mrs Minton, you've met Theodore's fiancée, haven't you? Mrs Rose Miles."

"Yes, I have done. It's a pleasure to see you again, Mrs Miles."

Rose thought it was tactful of Katherine Stone not to mention she had only met Mrs Minton because the Mintons' cook had been a possible source of information concerning a murder and a series of burglaries. It was possible Mrs Minton had never been enlightened as to why Rose had wanted a confidential word with her cook, and Rose was happy to keep her in ignorance.

So she merely murmured a polite reply and took the chair that Katherine indicated. Theo sat down beside her and said, "We were placing an order at the print shop in the High, and having got that far, we felt we should come the rest of the way and call on you."

"Whatever the reason, it is good to see you both. You must be half frozen, and I am sure hot tea would be welcome, would it not?"

"It would indeed," Theo said.

Hetty reappeared and was sent off to fetch two more cups and a fresh pot of tea.

"Is your writing going well, Theodore?" Mrs Minton asked.

"Very well, thank you. I admit I should be slaving away at my current book rather than taking tea with three charming ladies, but one cannot always have one's shoulder to the wheel."

"No, a break from duty is always welcome."

Theo suspected Mrs Minton had few duties in life beyond supervising her servants while they did the actual work, but he was too kind-hearted to say so. Besides, he wanted to turn the conversation around to see if either of the older women were familiar with any part of the Holt family.

Hetty came back with a replenished tray, and when she had gone and Theo and Rose had been supplied with tea, Katherine said, "What are you working on now, Theodore? Or is it to be kept secret until publication?"

Theo thought quickly. He hated to lie to his mother, but she had inadvertently given him a good opening, and he could always admit the truth later.

"Well, I had started on what I thought was a very imaginative plot, only to find my fanciful fiction had been overtaken by reality."

Both the older women were watching him, Mrs Minton with frank curiosity and his mother with a degree of justified skepticism.

"I had the idea of a man hailing a hansom cab, in perfect health, and being found dead in it at the end of his journey. And then my acquaintance at the police station, Inspector Reed, informed me that very event had happened here in Oxford only a few days ago. Not far from here, I believe. I was quite shocked."

"Oh, my goodness," Mrs Minton said, her eyes opening wide. "You are speaking of poor Timothy Holt, aren't you? A terrible tragedy."

"I'm afraid so," Theo said. "A tragedy indeed, and from what I have learned, the police are no nearer to learning who was responsible than they were a fortnight ago."

He didn't dare meet Katherine's eyes, nor Rose's. Rose, of course, knew perfectly well what he was doing, and he suspected his mother had guessed as well. Mrs Minton, blissfully unaware, was happy to discuss Holt's untimely death. It was probably the most interesting event she had heard about for some time.

"Such a dreadful thing to happen. I declare, the streets are simply not safe any more. Some ruffian must have attacked Mr Holt, perhaps thinking to rob him."

Theo noticed she had used the same term Reed said Mrs Holt had used. That indicated a possible conversation between the widow and Mrs Minton following Holt's death.

"Are you acquainted with the Holt family, Mrs Minton?" Rose asked, while Theo silently thanked her for picking up the cue. "If so, they must welcome your compassion in this distressing time."

"I have known Georgia Holt for years, and so of course, I called to express my condolences when I heard of the tragedy. It was difficult, however, to know what to say when a death had occurred in such … unusual … circumstances."

"Oh, I quite understand," Rose said. "The usual phrases must seem somehow trite and unhelpful. But I am certain Mrs Holt appreciated your thoughtfulness. Do the family live nearby?"

"Just two streets away. Stockmore Street. A very pleasant house, but of course, I don't know how they will manage now."

"Did Mr Holt not leave his family well provided for?" Theo asked. "I know we all think we are immortal, but after all, illness or accident – or crime – can cut anyone's lifespan short. It is best to be prepared."

"I don't know anything about finance," Mrs Minton said, falling back on the convenient fallacy, "but I understand his money was all invested in his business ventures. Poor

Georgia is having a great deal of difficulty extracting enough to even pay household expenses."

"How dreadful for her," Rose said. "I know, from my own experience, that a sudden unexpected death is hard enough to deal with, without additional burdens being heaped upon one. Are there no other family members who could help her?"

"Mr Holt's brother may possibly be able to offer some assistance, but he has his own affairs to tend to," Katherine said, making Theo wonder just how his mother was defining 'affairs'. It would be ironic if Gregory Holt couldn't assist his brother's family because he was financing his own mistress.

"And Georgia's own brother will be of little help." Mrs Minton's pursed lips showed her opinion of the man, so Theo was instantly intrigued.

"Oh? Why is that?"

"He lives in their house, but I'm afraid he doesn't contribute much. Not that he is a bad person," Mrs Minton added hastily, "but he is one of those who has great plans that never quite come to pass."

"A bit of a dreamer, then?" Rose asked.

"Yes, that is perhaps the kindest way of describing him."

"Well, one never knows," Theo said. "A year and a half ago, I was dreaming of becoming a successful writer, but not having much luck turning that dream into a reality. Then I met Rose, was accused of murder – which I didn't commit, incidentally – and had the idea of writing more popular fiction."

"And here you are, with your dream a reality and about to be married," Katherine said. "More tea, Rose?"

"Thank you."

"And then there are the children to consider," Mrs Minton said, her mind still on the financial plight of Timothy Holt's family. "The two older boys are away at school, but if the fees can't be met …"

"Perhaps Mrs Holt's brother will emulate Theo's success," Rose said, firmly steering the conversation back to the dreamer. "What is it that he wants to achieve?"

"I'm not actually certain. He claims to be an inventor, but as to what he is inventing – he's very vague on that subject."

"What is his name?" Theo asked. "I have encountered quite a few people of that sort, and may have heard of him."

"Shepherd. Daniel Shepherd."

Theo made a show of thinking deeply. "No, I don't believe I have done. A pity. Today's dreamer may be tomorrow's genius, with an invention or discovery to benefit the entire world."

"In this case, I rather doubt it," Katherine said. "But at least Mr Shepherd should be able to take on some responsibility and be a comfort to his sister. I have spoken to him a time or two. He is a pleasant enough man, but not terribly practical, one feels."

"So Mrs Holt may be the sort who willingly takes on responsibility in a difficult situation, do you think?" Rose asked.

"Oh, yes, I would say Georgia is very practical," Mrs Minton said. "She will cope with the situation in spite of the dreadful circumstances."

"Of course, I don't know her at all," Rose continued, "and will never have the opportunity of meeting Mr Holt and forming an opinion of him. What sort of person was he, can you tell us?"

"Very quiet, a bit abstracted, one might say, but always courteous."

That matched Mrs Preston's impression, although she had observed him under quite different circumstances. Theo found himself wondering how this quiet, serious man had stirred himself enough to acquire not only a wife, but a mistress as well.

And along with the wife, who had subsequently produced five children, a brother-in-law who appeared to contribute nothing but a drain on family resources.

"Did he get on with his brother-in-law?" Theo asked.

That was a crucial question, he knew. There was no reason to think Daniel Shepherd had driven a knife into his brother-in-law, but it would be helpful to know what the relationship between them had been. Had Holt resented the man who seemed to be living off the proceeds of someone else's business acumen? Even a quiet, courteous man could snap under pressure, and the two could have quarreled.

"I believe so," Mrs Minton said. "Although to be honest, I don't think they had much to do with each other. Mr Shepherd is almost always at the family home, whilst Mr Holt was always busy with his various enterprises and often away from home most of the day."

Theo didn't dare look at Rose, since they knew exactly where some of Timothy Holt's time and money had had been spent while away from the family home. From Mrs Minton's expression, she had no idea, or possibly, she couldn't believe he would be capable of such actions.

"I suppose it would be rather tactless of us to call on Mrs Holt, being as we have no previous acquaintance with the family," Theo said. "But if you should happen to call on her, Mother, I hope you will let her know Rose and I are thinking of her in this difficult time."

"Yes, I shall," Katherine said. "May I give you another cup of tea, Mrs Minton?"

Her guest looked at the clock on the wall and said, "No, thank you. I really must be getting back and speak to Cook about the evening meal. I believe Stephen has invited someone to dine with us, and that always means extra care must be taken to impress them."

"How true," Katherine said, while Theo reflected that neither of his parents had ever worried much about impressing anyone, even when they had invited Rose and her parents for a dinner party to mark their engagement. That had gone well enough, largely because Katherine found it easy to talk to anyone, a skill her eldest son had inherited.

"I hope your dinner guest proves entertaining," he said. "There are few things worse than suffering through a meal with a guest who has nothing of interest to contribute."

"I'm sure no one would ever say that of you, Theodore," Mrs Minton said, getting to her feet. "It was fortuitous, your having called whilst I was here, so I could reacquaint myself with Mrs Miles. I had been longing to do so." She gave Rose a smile signalling social approval before turning back to Theo. "And I hope your book progresses well, whether the plot comes from your imagination or real life."

"How kind of you to say so." Theo stood up and gave her a bow as Hetty held her coat for her.

They said their farewells, and when Mrs Minton had disappeared out the front door, Katherine looked at Theo.

"That was very cleverly done, Theodore," she said. "Are you and Rose somehow involved in the investigation into Timothy Holt's death? Because I don't believe for a second that you just happened to conjure up a plot that mimics a recent event as dramatic as that one."

"Are you suggesting a lack of imagination on my part, Mother?"

"No, I am suggesting you found a devious means of getting Mrs Minton to share information about the Holt family."

"You are far too clever," Theo said, with a grin. "Yes, you are quite correct. Do you have anything to add to the useful facts she supplied?"

Katherine reached for the teapot and refilled the cups. "Besides the useful facts that the family may be suffering financially following Timothy Holt's death, and that his brother-in-law is unlikely to contribute much either in the form of funds or emotional support?"

"Besides that, yes. I gathered you are not as familiar with Mrs Holt as Mrs Minton is."

"No, I am not. I know who she is and have exchanged greetings, but not much beyond that."

"I spoke to father earlier and he told me that although he had heard of them, he had never actually met either of the Holt brothers. Does that mean they are amongst those who look down on 'trade'?"

"Possibly. I've never inquired."

"And Mr Shepherd? You said you had spoken to him a time or two."

"An inoffensive man. An almost colorless personality. I have no idea what his opinion is of income derived from trade, considering that he does not appear to actually work at anything."

"I see."

"You did not answer my first question, you know," Katherine said sternly. "Are you involved in investigating Timothy Holt's death? I can think of no other reason for you to show such interest. It was a tragedy for the family, and a puzzling thing to have happened, but I am inclined to agree he was a victim of street crime. A robbery that went wrong, perhaps. Or am I totally mistaken?"

Theo leaned back in his armchair while he debated how much to share with his mother. Of course, when he returned home that evening, his father would mention Theo's visit to the brewery and his questions about the Holt brothers. However, he wouldn't have heard about Bellamy's death. There was not much reason, Theo concluded, to dodge the issue.

"Yes, to both questions," he said. "We are investigating his death, alongside the police, and although I can't say for certain, I strongly suspect you and Mrs Minton are both mistaken about it being the result of street crime."

"Why is that?"

"Because the driver of the hansom cab in which Timothy Holt died was himself the victim of a fatal stabbing, earlier this afternoon. The exact same technique was used, and I cannot believe that was coincidence. Neither can the police."

He watched his mother with some concern, but Katherine Stone was not the kind of woman to need smelling salts on receiving shocking news. A sharp intake of breath and a widening of her eyes were the only indications of her reaction to Theo's statement.

"Oh, my gracious," she said. "Thank heavens you didn't tell Mrs Minton about that, or she would never venture out of her front door again. And she would certainly never dare travel in a cab. The poor man. Where did it happen?"

"He died more or less in the midst of the High Street, although the police feel the attack itself must have taken place a little further away, at Carfax, a few minutes earlier. It took him a while to bleed to death."

Katherine's face was grave. "And that is almost what happened to Timothy Holt, isn't it? From what I understand, he must have been attacked at the start of his journey. Of course, the natural supposition was that his assailant was someone on the street – probably someone who attempted to rob him and when rebuffed, stabbed him."

"How do you know they were rebuffed?" Rose asked curiously.

"Because a purse in his pocket still contained money when he was found in the cab."

"Oh," Theo said. "That's interesting. Inspector Reed didn't tell me that. How did you find out, Mother? No, don't bother – it was Mrs Minton, wasn't it?"

"I'm afraid so. She went to call on Mrs Holt and whilst expressing her condolences, Mrs Holt remarked that at least he hadn't been robbed, although that was of course a minor consolation."

"No doubt. One would think, however, that having stabbed him fatally, a thief would not have scrupled to take whatever money or purse he could find."

"You would think so, yes," Katherine said. "And I imagine there are a number of dubious characters in Beaumont Street at any given time, even though it is quite a respectable area."

Theo and Rose exchanged glances and Theo said, "How do you know that is where he hailed the cab? Was that piece of information revealed by Mrs Holt as well?"

He took it for granted that she had not read the newspaper account, his parents being traditional enough to believe women had no need to learn about current events, or at least as reported in the press.

Katherine didn't reply immediately and Theo had the impression he had asked the wrong question. Or more likely, the right one, but his mother was reluctant to answer it.

"You understand," she said finally, "I would not speak of this to anyone but you and Rose, and trust you will not repeat it."

"No, we won't," Theo said, and Rose nodded in agreement.

"I'm afraid it was known that Timothy Holt kept a young mistress in a house not far from Beaumont Street. He had been seen there a number of times and one assumes that is where he had been – calling on her – just before he was attacked."

ELEVEN

Theo reflected how very accurate Mrs Preston had been when she said people snooped and gossiped. His mother, living on the other side of Oxford and not even a close friend of Georgia Holt's, had heard of her husband's extramarital affair, to the extent of knowing more or less where Irene Appleby lived. No wonder it hadn't taken the police long to locate her.

"As it happens," he said, "you needn't worry about our discretion. That piece of information is already known to us, and in fact, that is how we have become involved. The young woman in question was being held by the police in connection with Mr Holt's death, and we were asked to try and clear her name."

To her credit, Katherine showed no negative reaction to the idea that the Milestone Agency was working on behalf of a young woman of questionable morals. She merely looked at Theo and said, "Where is she being held?"

"Oxford Prison."

"Is she still there?"

"Possibly not now. Because …"

"Because if she was in prison at the time, she could not also be at Carfax stabbing a cab driver, and it appears the police believe the same person committed both crimes."

"Precisely. I believe Inspector Reed will be releasing her this afternoon, or tomorrow at the latest."

"I am glad to hear that, despite her relationship with Mr Holt. I can't in good conscience approve of that, but it doesn't mean she was responsible for his death. What reason did the police have for thinking her guilty?"

"She was a convenient suspect. Their theory was that she may have had a better offer from someone else and Mr Holt refused to let her go. And unfortunately for her, she has no viable alibi for the time when he was killed. She was not at home but refuses to say where she was, only that she was meeting with someone."

"How foolish of her," Katherine said. "Have you met this young woman, Theodore, and spoken to her? I assume you have done, if you are working on her behalf."

"We held a short conversation in the prison this morning. Not the best surroundings, to be sure, but it was rather illuminating."

"And what sort of person is she? I am not speaking of her morals, since she may have had no choice but to accept his protection, but her character. Her personality."

Theo thought for a moment, remembering the impression Irene Appleby had made on him, allowing for the negative circumstances.

"She is very attractive, reasonably intelligent, and in a different setting, I imagine she could be quite charming. She told me she was a foundling, raised in an orphanage, and it seems that has given her a certain resilience of character. She wouldn't have gone to her fate without a fight, I am sure."

"So you believe her to be innocent?"

"Yes, I do. Having said that, she is not helping matters by refusing to provide an alibi."

"No, I can see that. So it is either something she is very ashamed of, or she is trying to protect someone else."

"I believe we shall have to recruit you to our agency, Mother," Theo said. "That is more or less what we had decided, although I can't imagine anything so embarrassing that she would rather be hanged than admit it."

"Can't you? But then, you are a man."

Katherine looked at Rose, who said quietly, "Perhaps she had found she was with child and wanted to … be rid of it. That would be not only embarrassing, but dangerous and illegal. And she would hardly tell anyone where she was going, even if it was only to make inquiries about the possibility."

"Oh."

"Although it might be something far less damaging. Unless she will tell us, we can only guess."

"And we may not be anywhere near the truth," Theo said. "Mother, I know you have only a superficial knowledge of Georgia Holt, but do you think she was aware of her husband's activities? It seems everyone else was."

"I honestly don't know," Katherine said. "I would suspect she was aware of it. Of course, if she was, she would never admit it publicly, perhaps not even to close friends. I am certainly not privy to the state of their marriage, except to observe that Mr Holt must have found it unsatisfactory in some aspect."

"That's a polite but accurate way of expressing it," Theo said. "However, I have to say that Mrs Minton didn't seem to know of Mr Holt's mistress. Or do you think she was simply ignoring the fact in the way that ladies would be expected to?"

Katherine smiled. "Mrs Minton thinks the best of everyone, which may be commendable but not very practical. If she had been given the name and address of Timothy Holt's paramour, she would still find an alternative explanation for him having gone there. Speaking of which, can you tell me – what is the young woman's name? I can't keep referring to her with euphemisms."

Theo hesitated and then said, "Appleby. Irene Appleby."

"And she asked you to act on her behalf?"

"No, she did not. Her servants are very concerned about her, and one of them consulted us without her knowledge. We agreed to look into the matter. Of course, that was before the second murder, which rather changes the picture."

"So your part in the matter may be finished," Katherine said. "You would, I suppose, like to know who did kill Timothy Holt, if it was not his mistress. And I imagine she would like to know, too."

"Yes, we would. I assume his family would as well, although they are not likely to welcome our assistance."

"No. That would be admitting the existence of Miss Appleby." Katherine thought for a moment and then said, "I find it encouraging that her servants were so concerned about her, even if it was because they feared losing their posts if she was convicted of murder. One can get a fairly accurate idea of character by what the staff think of their employers."

Rose considered her own servants in regard to that theory. She had always got along well with Cora, who had been with her since before her marriage to Edward. Cook approved of her because she left the running of the kitchen to someone who knew what she was doing. Rose had engaged several different house and kitchen maids, young girls who worked for a while and then left to get married or take a post in a grander household. None of them had expressed any dissatisfaction with her, at least not openly.

As for Pickett, he had adjusted calmly to his new role as butler and bodyguard, and she thought he was genuinely concerned about her welfare. That, rather than snobbery, was why he had been reluctant at first to accept that Theo's interest was in her, not her bank account.

It would be gratifying to think that if for some reason she had found herself in as much jeopardy as Irene Appleby, her servants would rally round to her defense as Irene's had done. And that was even without someone as determined as Mrs Preston on her staff.

"Yes, they apparently were all entirely convinced of her innocence, which now looks more probable," Theo said. "After all, her charwoman who came to us made a good point. Why would she kill the man who was providing her with a reasonable lifestyle?"

"A good question," Katherine said. "What will you do next?"

"I'm not certain," Theo admitted. "As we've said, the cab driver's murder has completely changed the picture."

"Well, not completely," Rose reminded him. "We are assuming the two deaths are connected and now two potential suspects in Mr Holt's death have been eliminated. Permanently, in poor Mr Bellamy's case."

"That is the cab driver?" Katherine asked.

"Yes," Theo said. "He must have seen or said something that posed a danger to Mr Holt's attacker. Or it may be that they only *thought* he posed a danger to them. I imagine that if you have successfully carried off one murder, you would be forever looking over your shoulder, wondering if you left a clue to your identity somewhere. But to answer your original question, I hope to be able to speak to Gregory Holt about his brother before long, and possibly to his solicitor as well. Miss Appleby seemed to think they were friends as well as solicitor and client."

"And of course, we will be speaking to Miss Appleby again," Rose said. "I am sure she would not have wanted someone else to die in order to vindicate her, but once out of prison, she may feel she can speak more freely."

"I wish you success then," Katherine said. "And if you take a cab back to St Giles, please be vigilant."

To be honest, Theo was not at all keen about embarking on a journey by hansom cab, but neither did he want to walk all the way back to St Giles in the chilly, rapidly darkening afternoon. A look at Rose confirmed she felt the same way.

"We don't pose any threat to anyone," Theo said, trying to convince himself. "And we probably know less about both deaths than the police do. It's cold; it's a long way, too far to walk. Let's hail a cab."

"Yes, I think walking back to St Giles would be taking caution a bit too far."

They did start the journey on foot, however, and were nearly to the Plain when an empty cab rolled past them and Theo hailed it. He held the door for Rose and took the precaution of looking all around before getting in and sitting beside her. By an unspoken mutual consent, they didn't say a word about the events of the day as they rode, or discuss their conversations at the Stone residence.

Theo had asked the driver to take them to the crossroads just before Rose's house, not wanting to give the exact number. They disembarked and again, he looked around cautiously, but saw no one lurking with malicious intent. He paid the driver, the cab moved off and he heaved a sigh of relief.

"We will have to resolve this case or we will never feel comfortable riding in a cab again," he said, as they went to the door. "Perhaps we shall have to resort to keeping a carriage."

"I don't think it will be that bad," Rose said, as Pickett opened the door to them. "Are you joining me for supper?"

"If you don't mind, I will. I think we need to mull over Mrs Minton's contributions."

Theo noted with some amusement that Rose's cook now assumed he would be eating most of his evening meals with her, and had prepared enough food for both of them. He hoped his own landlady had made the same assumption and had not stretched the curry or stew – her two standby meals – far enough to feed him as well as the other man who rented rooms from her.

They went into the dining room and over the cutlets and vegetables, recounted the events of the afternoon. This led to a depressing conclusion.

"We really are not much further forward, are we?" Theo said. "The only definite fact we have learned is that William Bellamy can be removed from suspicion for Mr Holt's murder. And even that depends on the theory that the same person was responsible for both deaths."

"I think they must be. It would simply be too much of a coincidence otherwise. I should think cab drivers are a fairly tough breed, and Mr Bellamy would not have simply stood still and let someone stab him. He must have been identified by his assailant first and then somehow distracted enough for the attack to take place."

"Yes, since it's hard to believe anyone would stab a cab driver at random. He was their target, and probably for the reasons we said before. He knew too much, or could identify Mr Holt's attacker."

"In that case," Rose said, "why didn't Mr Bellamy recognize the person? I realize he must encounter a great number of persons during an average day, but as you say, he wouldn't have simply stood there if he knew it was the same person he'd seen in Beaumont Street just before Mr Holt got into his cab."

"That's a very good point," Theo said. "Were they somehow disguised, do you think?"

"Or perhaps so nondescript that he didn't take any notice of them," Rose said thoughtfully. "Both Carfax and Beaumont streets tend to be busy, with all sorts of people there, especially Carfax."

That was undeniably true. The crossroads at the heart of Oxford was nearly always crowded with both vehicles and pedestrians, ranging from small children trying to sell bootlaces to elegantly dressed residents riding in their carriages. Somewhere in between were workmen, black-gowned undergraduate students from the colleges, and housewives going to or from shops or the large covered market.

Beaumont Street, home to the surgeries of several doctors and dentists, was less crowded, but still busy. On the corner where it met St Giles, the impressive Randolph Hotel and the Ashmolean Museum guaranteed a steady stream of passers-by. Timothy Holt might have hailed Bellamy's cab there for that very reason – to not be noticed.

Someone had known he was there, however. And in Beaumont Street, as in Carfax, a knife-wielding killer had managed to blend into the background both before and after dispatching their victim.

"Since we are not likely to have any success finding witnesses to either attack," Theo said, "I believe the key to resolving this is to discover the motive for Timothy Holt's murder. We must ask ourselves who is better off – in terms of money, satisfaction or safety – following his death?"

"Safety?" Rose asked, lifting her eyebrows.

"He could have learned a fact about someone which they didn't want to be revealed. I can't see him stooping to blackmail, but he might not have needed to. Just the possibility of their secret becoming public may have terrified the person."

Rose thought about that, trying to imagine what secret could be terrible enough to motivate someone to commit two murders.

"You could be right," she said doubtfully, "but from what we've been told about Mr Holt, I'm more inclined to think money is at the root of his murder. So if you can see his friend the solicitor, perhaps you can extract some details from him. Who benefits from his death, for example. I should think it would be his wife and children, but people have been known to make very strange wills."

"They certainly have done," Theo said with feeling "Let us hope that Mr Holt wasn't moved by some impulse to leave all his money to Irene Appleby. That would, as they say, set the cat amongst the pigeons. Even leaving it all to some obscure charity would be better."

"I hope his solicitor will be able to perhaps confirm whether his will was an orthodox one. I suppose he might have made some bequest to her, a modest amount, but he was unlikely to let her know what he'd done. If he was only in his forties, he could be expected to live for some time, and one feels she was better off with him alive."

Cora came to clear the table and inquire about serving dessert. "It's treacle tart, ma'am, with custard if you want."

"Yes, please, but no custard for me. Mr Stone?" Even as she spoke, Rose wondered why she felt obliged to be so formal when the servants were listening. After they were married, she hoped she might be able to call him Theo.

"Yes, please, and custard as well," Theo said. When Cora had gone he said, "I always feel as though treacle tart is pulling my teeth out, it's so sticky, but I do love it."

"I'm sure that is why Cook made it. She knows you like it and you have charmed her completely with your praise."

"Praise which is sincerely meant. It has taken Mrs Rice's well-meaning but insipid meals to make me truly appreciate good cooking."

Cora came back with dishes of the golden brown dessert under its cross-hatched crust, setting a small pitcher of warm custard beside Theo's place.

"That looks extremely tasty," he said. "My compliments to Cook."

"Yes, sir." Cora blushed and fled to the kitchen.

"Do I make her nervous?" Theo asked Rose.

"Possibly. She's very excited about the wedding and moving to a new house."

"As am I. Willows is coming along well and I think we'll be able to move in by the end of February, at the latest."

"That is excellent news," Rose said. "I've almost been afraid to inquire, in case there was some major hurdle to be overcome."

"No, it's all been straightforward. And I imagine I should go there after finishing this marvelous pudding and work on my book. With luck, I'll have an hour or more to write before I need to head back to my rooms."

Rose smiled at him. She knew he would prefer to spend the rest of the evening – and probably the night as well – with her, but his publisher was eager to receive his latest manuscript. As Theo had regretfully noted on more than one occasion, books did not write themselves, regardless of what the reading public believed.

When the dessert plates were cleared and they had gone back to the drawing room, Theo retrieved his coat and hat and put them on, ready to walk to Willows. He kissed Rose and said, "I will see you tomorrow and we can decide what we need to do next. I shouldn't be at all surprised to see Mrs Preston on the doorstep, thanking us …"

He stopped, because Pickett had opened the door and coughed discreetly, causing Theo to loosen his hold on Rose's shoulders.

"Pardon, ma'am, but there is someone at the door, asking to see you and Mr Stone."

"I told you so," Theo said. "Who is it, Pickett?"

"A young woman, sir. She gave her name as Miss Appleby."

TWELVE

Theo's first thought was that he was not going to be writing anything for a while, because he was extremely curious to know what Irene Appleby was doing at Rose's door. He supposed she had been speedily released from prison, gone home to wash, change her clothes and have something to eat, and then had learned Rose's address from Mrs Preston.

That was all very well, but it must be something urgent to bring her there in the evening rather than waiting for the next day.

"Ask her to come in," Rose said. Theo took his hat and coat off and laid them on an armchair as Pickett ushered their caller in.

Irene Appleby looked much better than she had the previous time Theo had seen her. She had washed her face and brushed her auburn hair, pinning it up neatly under her hat. She was wearing a dress that fit well under a warm wool coat. Had he known nothing of her background, he would have placed her as the wife, daughter or sister of a solidly middle-class man. It was not so much the clothing, he realized, as her manner – far more confident and self-assured now.

Rose had no previous image to compare, but she instantly realized why Timothy Holt must have been attracted to her. Irene was not only lovely, but looked as though she would smile easily and be a cheerful companion. At the moment, however, her face was serious and with a jolt of recognition, Rose noted that her coat, dress and hat were all black. She was wearing mourning for the man who had been an important part of her life and didn't care who knew it.

Theo cleared his throat and said, "I am glad to see you are at liberty, Miss Appleby. I am not sure introductions are necessary, but if they are …"

"I'm Rose Miles," Rose said quickly. "I daresay Mr Stone mentioned me when he spoke to you earlier."

"Yes, he did. I'm sorry to call on you at this hour, Mrs Miles, but I felt I should speak to you and Mr Stone. Inspector Reed said I might find you both here."

"Bless him," Theo said. "Yes, I am often here, for both business and personal reasons, as Mrs Miles and I are engaged to be married."

"Oh, I see. My congratulations to you both."

Irene smiled and Rose wondered what would have happened if Theo had left the house a few minutes earlier. Would she have felt comfortable speaking to a woman whose life had been funded by a man married to someone else? Or would she have asked Irene to come back in the morning when Theo was present?

That was irrelevant now. Rose gestured to a chair and said, "Please have a seat, Miss Appleby, and tell us what is on your mind. It must be serious, to bring you here in the evening."

"Yes, it is, or at least I feel that it is." Irene sat down, sweeping her skirts under her with a graceful gesture. "I apologize for intruding, but the more I thought about it, the more I felt I must speak to you."

"Go ahead," Theo said.

Irene cleared her throat and said, "Inspector Reed came to the prison late this afternoon and instructed the governor to release me. He said no charges would be brought, but that I was not to leave Oxford. I never intended to, so that was no hardship. He would not tell me why he suddenly changed his mind about my possible guilt. It occurred to me that you may know the reason, so I thought I would ask. Do you?"

Theo and Rose looked at each other.

"Inspector Reed gave you no clue, no explanation at all?" Theo asked.

"None."

"I don't know why he didn't, but since you will find out sooner or later, I may as well tell you. A second man died today, attacked in exactly the same manner as Mr Holt was. Since you obviously could not have committed that crime, and the two attacks were identical, the police deduced you were not responsible for Mr Holt's death, either."

Irene sat very still, absorbing Theo's announcement.

"How dreadful," she said in a voice that was barely above a whisper. "Can you tell me who the second man was?"

"A man called William Bellamy."

"William Bellamy," she repeated, sounding mildly puzzled.

"A hansom cab driver. He was the man who drove the cab Mr Holt died in."

"Oh, no." The color drained from Irene's face. Theo went to the sideboard and poured a small measure of brandy into a glass.

"Drink this," he told her. "You're as pale as a ghost."

That brought a faint smile and she sipped the brandy. "Thank you, Mr Stone. I'm sorry; it was just such a shock. That poor man – was he killed because he drove Timothy in his cab? Perhaps because of something he saw or heard?"

"Quite possibly."

"Oh, dear."

She was obviously thinking the matter over, so neither Theo nor Rose said anything. She finished the brandy and set the glass on a small table.

"I had no idea," she said. "I thought perhaps the police had found some evidence that convinced them I had nothing to do with Timothy's death. I can hardly believe they released me because someone else was killed."

"That is the reason," Rose said. "For heaven's sake, Miss Appleby, don't blame yourself, if that is what you are thinking. You could have done nothing to prevent Mr Bellamy's death. Nothing, that is, unless you knew who had killed Mr Holt but failed to tell the police."

For a moment, she thought she had penetrated Irene's defenses. Their eyes met and Irene's were almost pleading. Then she dropped her gaze.

"I can see I made a mistake in coming here," she said quietly.

"How so?" Theo asked.

"I was simply intending to ask whether you knew why I had been released. And then I was going to thank you for your efforts so far and suggest that you leave the investigation into Timothy's death to the police. But now …"

"The situation has become more complicated, hasn't it?" Rose said. "Two men are dead, probably by the same hand, and unless I am mistaken, you know something that might help in finding who killed them."

"But I can't …" Irene seemed on the verge of tears, but then got herself under control. "Please don't look into this any further. As you say, Mrs Miles, two men have already lost their lives. Don't make it any worse."

Before either Theo or Rose could think of an appropriate response, she stood up, gave them a tentative smile and started for the door. Theo almost jumped to get there ahead of her and opened it.

Pickett was in the hallway and Theo wondered how much he had heard. He turned to Irene and said, "Should you change your mind, you know where to find us. Pickett, if

Miss Appleby calls again, she is to be admitted, any time of day or night."

"Yes, sir." Pickett's tone was resigned, as if deploring a caller who had no idea of the proper time to appear.

"Thank you," Irene said. "Good night, Mr Stone."

"Good night."

Theo stood in the doorway watching until Irene had disappeared from sight. He went back to the drawing room and said to Rose, "Now, what on earth do we make of that?"

"Two things, I suppose. She didn't know William Bellamy, and hadn't been told of his death. She does know something about Mr Holt's death that she is holding back. And thirdly – I have no idea how to persuade her to divulge it."

"I am forced to agree on all three points. Ah well, I shall go to my writing desk now, submerge myself in fiction for a while, and tomorrow morning we will tackle this problem anew. I have a suggestion."

"What is it?"

"I will try and see either Gregory Holt or the solicitor tomorrow, whichever will agree to speak to me. You might wander by Holy Trinity church and see if by chance Mrs Preston is about. She may not be, since Miss Appleby is home again, but then again, she may be doing a final stint there. if she is, perhaps she could contribute some details of Miss Appleby's return."

"A good idea. I don't think I should go to her house. Let her come to us again, if she will. But I have had another thought."

"Yes?"

"Since she has asked us not to pursue the matter, are we being foolish in ignoring her request?"

"I don't honestly know," Theo said. "I hate to just drop it without resolution, especially since we have no idea why she doesn't want us to continue. It almost sounded as if she expected someone else to be murdered if we did."

"Yes," Rose said. "And that could be a real possibility. Someone who has already killed twice probably would not worry about further victims. The problem is identifying who those potential victims might be – who they believe might still pose a danger to them."

"If she persists in holding back vital information, it may well be Miss Appleby," Theo said soberly. "I hope she realizes that." He picked up his coat and hat again and put them on. "Good night, then, my dear, and I shall see you tomorrow."

After Theo had gone, Rose sat down in the drawing room and went over what Irene Appleby had said. And more importantly, what she hadn't said. It was clear that she knew something that might hold a key to Timothy Holt's murder, and equally clear that she wasn't going to reveal it.

She might eventually have said something, if the alternative was the gallows, but now that she had been released from prison and no charges brought against her, it seemed unlikely. Her freedom had been bought at the price of William Bellamy's death. Would that make her feel guilty enough to let go of her secret?

Rose sighed, wishing she had the sort of insight that might let her understand what Irene was thinking. But her own circumstances were so different that she couldn't begin to imagine what would be so important to her that she would keep it secret in this situation.

Theo was also thinking of Irene Appleby. Whatever she was concealing had to be concerned with the meeting she had gone to while Timothy Holt was being fatally stabbed. That indicated someone didn't want her to have a provable alibi for the time in question. But that argued two people were involved – one to lure Irene into a vulnerable position and the other to attack Holt.

Theo stared at his manuscript. There was something of a parallel in his current plot, a man who had been framed for a crime and then tossed to the wolves when he was no longer needed. Irene had served her purpose as a suspect, so what would happen to her now?

He thought it was rather careless of Bellamy's killer not to have realized that Irene couldn't be in two places at once and that the similarity of the two murders would set alarms ringing in Inspector Reed's mind. That argued that either they had underestimated the police, or that they were desperate to silence Bellamy.

And why the two-week gap between the two deaths? If they had decided Bellamy must die, had it taken a fortnight to identify or locate him? Or had some new event triggered the second murder?

Theo picked up his pen and began to write.

The following morning, Theo was awake and dressed at an hour he previously would have thought impossible. This was largely because he felt he needed to get his thoughts in order before seeking an audience with either Gregory Holt or Bernard Caldwell.

Caldwell, he felt, would be easier to locate, because a solicitor would have to have an official presence somewhere. From what his father had said, Gregory Holt could be anywhere and might not even have a permanent place of work.

Accordingly, he presented himself at the table almost before Mrs Rice had finished grilling the kippers and buttering the bread for his breakfast. She put the plate in front of him and poured a cup of tea.

"I hope you're not off to prison again today, Mr Stone," she said.

"No, I'm not. I'm hoping to see a solicitor."

Mrs Rice frowned, because in her world, anything and anyone associated with the law meant bad news.

"Oh, dear."

"Not to act for me, Mrs Rice. I simply want some information from him."

"That's all right, then."

Theo finished his breakfast and set off for the center of Oxford. His first destination was the chambers of the solicitors who drew up contracts and other legal documents for the family brewery. If Bernard Caldwell practiced law in Oxford, Theo reasoned they might know of him, and if not, would at least know where to find him.

This proved to be the case, and less than an hour later, Theo was in possession of an address culled from a list of local solicitors and barristers. He stood outside the building in question for a moment, trying to formulate an approach that would not see him thrown out for wasting Caldwell's time, or worse, keep him from being admitted in the first place.

He knew better than to claim an acquaintance with any member of the Holt family, or to pretend he had any official backing from the police, so that only left one realistic choice. He entered the office, summoned up the most officious manner he could muster, and said, "I should like to see Mr Caldwell, if he can spare me a few minutes. My name is Stone, and I represent Miss Irene Appleby."

The clerk at the desk gave an almost audible gulp and surveyed Theo from the top of his best hat to his polished boots.

"If you'll wait here a moment, Mr Stone, I'll see if he can offer you an appointment."

"It's imperative I see him as soon as possible," Theo said. He considered softening the demand with a smile and decided against it.

"Yes, sir, I'll inquire."

The clerk fled through a door and Theo looked around him. The office was small, but the furniture was of good quality, the room immaculate and the clerk, although nervous, seemed competent enough. He deduced that Bernard Caldwell was no shyster, but a respectable member of the bar.

The clerk returned and said, "Mr Caldwell said he can give you a few minutes, Mr Stone, but he has a client expected at ten o'clock."

"Thank you." It was now a quarter to ten, but Theo reckoned it would only take a few minutes to make some preliminary inquiries, and since he had fully expected to be turned away, he wasn't inclined to quibble.

Caldwell was seated behind a mahogany desk, the opposite wall covered completely by a glass-fronted bookcase filled with leather-bound volumes. He was a man of perhaps fifty, very thin, clean-shaven, and with spectacles perched on his nose. Theo's impression was that any normal emotions had been drained out of him, leaving only intellect. He looked at Theo as if inspecting the details of a questionable legal case.

"Thank you for seeing me, Mr Caldwell," Theo said quickly.

"Sit down." It was an order and Theo obeyed, settling himself in a straight-backed wooden chair. "My clerk told me you represent Miss Irene Appleby."

"Yes, I do. More or less."

"So which is it? More, or less?"

Theo took a deep breath. "I suppose you would call it less, since she does not know I am here. I represent an investigative agency hired to clear Miss Appleby's name in the matter of Timothy Holt's murder. She told me you were a friend of Mr Holt's, in addition, perhaps, to acting for him in a professional capacity."

He paused, to allow comment, but received only a nod.

"So I assume you have an interest from both points of view in finding out who was responsible for his death. It was not Miss Appleby. The police have now determined she played no part in it and her name has been cleared."

"So why are you here, Mr Stone, if what you were hired for has been accomplished?"

"Because Mr Holt's killer has not yet been apprehended, and it seems likely that money or the expectation of it played a part in his death. Therefore, we feel we can't simply drop the matter, even though, as you say, our direct involvement has ended. I don't expect you to divulge details, but I wondered if you could tell me whether Miss Appleby benefits at all from Mr Holt's will. That is, I assumed you had drawn one up for him. If you didn't, I apologize for wasting your time."

Caldwell surveyed him in much the same manner as the clerk had, but obviously for a different reason. Theo could almost see him calculating how far he could be trusted and what ulterior motive he might have.

"You are quite correct, in that I cannot divulge details," he said finally. "But I can tell you that Miss Appleby does not benefit from Timothy Holt's will. She has no need to."

THIRTEEN

That statement left Theo mildly puzzled, wondering what exactly Caldwell meant. The logical conclusion was that Timothy Holt had not expected to die for some years to come, so perhaps had provided Irene with substantial funds in the short term. That would be in addition, he supposed, to the amount he gave her to pay her day-to-day expenses.

He was rather glad to learn she had no financial motive for murdering him, not that he had thought she had. But how far had Holt's generosity extended? And perhaps more importantly, who else knew about it? Would Irene herself now become a target?

"Are you perhaps saying that his death made no difference to her financially?" he asked tentatively. "That possibly he had already made arrangements to secure her future?"

"You may conclude that, yes."

Theo supposed that meant money deposited in a bank account or in some investment that would benefit her. And it would be in her name, not his, to safeguard it. The will would not mention her at all. As Irene herself had said, she didn't exist in the eyes of Holt's family, even if they were aware of the role she had played in his life.

"So I assume the terms of Mr Holt's will were what one might expect," he said, "providing for his widow and children."

"Yes."

"Thank you, Mr Caldwell. That is really all I wanted to know – or confirm – and I appreciate you taking the time to see me."

"Mr Stone."

"Yes, sir?"

"I can perhaps save you some time if I tell you that Miss Appleby was fully aware she would not benefit from Mr Holt's death. Timothy Holt himself told me he had made it clear to her and she accepted that."

Theo couldn't help smiling. "Yes, indeed. I know she didn't play a part in his death, but I am glad to hear that she knew she wouldn't have benefitted financially, if there had been any doubt in the matter. Thank you again, sir."

He started to stand up and then remembered Caldwell might be of some further use, so sat back down.

"You have been so obliging, Mr Caldwell, that I hesitate to ask another favor of you, but I had hoped to speak to Gregory Holt regarding his brother. Do you know where I might find him?"

"You will be fortunate to locate him at any given time," Caldwell said. "Are you aware of what he does?"

"I have been told he – and Timothy Holt as well – provide funds for prospective businesses, those which they feel show promise. One or both of the brothers would invest in the business and then share in the profits if it was successful. Or, I imagine, share in the loss if it were not."

Theo saw no need to tell Caldwell his father had supplied that useful piece of information. Let the solicitor think the Milestone Agency was both competent and discreet.

"Yes," Caldwell said. "One could characterize it as a gamble, but I believe they were quite expert at gauging the likelihood of success or failure. Anyway, Gregory Holt has no permanent office that I know of, largely operating from his home. But he is constantly moving about, speaking to people, visiting businesses he has helped fund, and so on."

Theo sighed, thinking Caldwell was probably right in thinking he would be lucky to catch such an active man. After all, Gregory had been proven to be in the town of Banbury, several miles away, at the time his brother was killed. That showed that not only did he cover a great deal of territory, but could definitely be eliminated as a suspect.

"I understand he lives in Banbury Road; do you know if that is correct?"

"Yes."

"Do you happen to know which …"

"An enterprise such as the Holt brothers run involves a certain number of legal documents," Caldwell said, sounding slightly amused. "Of course his house number has occasionally appeared on those documents, but you will understand you did not learn it from me."

"Certainly not." Theo felt that Caldwell might, after all, be human, rather than the dry stick he had first appeared to be. Being given Holt's address would save having to wander up and down a very long street trying to find the correct number.

"Assuming I provide you with the number, what do you expect to learn from him?"

"Whether he knows of anyone who would be better off with Timothy Holt dead, and may have had the opportunity to make that happen."

"Someone other than Miss Appleby, who has been ruled out, and in any case, would not benefit. As I understand it, Mr Stone, that is what you hoped to learn from me and I have confirmed it."

Caldwell appeared to be thinking over their conversation, so Theo waited patiently, hoping the ten o'clock client wouldn't be early for their appointment or that the solicitor would feel he had already revealed enough.

"I have never met Miss Appleby," he said finally, "but I know she meant a great deal to Timothy Holt. And yes, he was a friend of mine, and I should like to see whoever killed him to be brought to justice. I don't know how deeply you and your agency are involved in this matter, Mr Stone, but if you are fortunate, you may find Gregory Holt at number 77 Banbury Road."

"Thank you very much, Mr Caldwell. I do appreciate your help. And I hope to be instrumental in finding whoever was responsible for your friend's death. May I leave my card with you, in the event you wish to contact me?"

He took a business card from his pocket, and after a brief hesitation, Caldwell took it and put it in the top drawer of his desk. Then he touched a button which rang a bell in the reception area. The clerk appeared in the doorway; Caldwell stood up and Theo shook hands with him before following the clerk out.

At roughly the same time Theo was leaving Caldwell's office, Rose was walking toward Holy Trinity Church, hoping to catch Mrs Preston before she returned full-time to her post with Irene Appleby.

She was not on her own, however, having asked Cora to come with her. It was not simply a matter of giving Cora a break from her duties or having a companion to lessen the chances of being set upon by someone hoping to rob a well-dressed woman.

Rose had suddenly had the idea that Mrs Preston might confide details to Cora that she would hesitate to tell Rose. After all, they were more on the same social level, and if Mrs Preston was at the church, Cora would feel comfortable talking to her there, having – unlike Rose – attended services at Holy Trinity most Sundays.

So as they walked, Rose provided Cora with enough background to enable her to ask pertinent questions if the occasion arose. She had been a little hesitant about describing

Timothy Holt's role in Irene Appleby's life, but she needn't have worried. Although Cora might be somewhat vague on the precise details, she understood that gentlemen had needs that their wives didn't always fulfill, and that they might use the services of other women, either on a temporary or semi-permanent basis, to compensate.

"My ma told me about that sort of thing when I went into service," she reassured Rose. "Told me to always be careful, 'cause men can't be trusted and it's easy for a girl to lose her reputation and never get it back. But this Miss Appleby, she weren't a dolly mop or jade off the street Mr Holt'd just used, were she? Not if he gave her a house and servants and all."

"No, she isn't, and I think there was a fair amount of mutual affection as well," Rose said. "Of course, he couldn't marry her, since he was already married."

"Pity. Wonder if he would have done, if his missus weren't there."

Rose looked at Cora, whose expression indicated complete innocence of what that might imply. She had to admit it was an intriguing question. Having now met Irene, she could see that she was not an illiterate serving girl, but an intelligent, articulate woman who might in time have been accepted as Holt's wife. That was assuming, of course, that Georgia Holt died in a timely and respectable manner and the couple had been prepared to ignore the inevitable sniping that would have followed their marriage.

But what if the situation had been reversed? Was it remotely possible that Holt's death had cleared the way for Georgia Holt to marry someone else? For a moment, Rose felt inexplicably guilty, knowing that if she had met Theo while Edward was alive, she still would have been attracted to him. She wouldn't have pursued the attraction, of course, but in a similar situation, Georgia might have felt differently. To the point of murder? It seemed unlikely, but was just possible.

Everything they had heard so far indicated no grievous flaws in Timothy Holt, except for his interest in Irene Appleby. Even if Georgia Holt had been aware of Irene's presence in her husband's life, as his wife she held the upper hand, so to speak, both legally and morally. Holt had provided for his family, given his wife a home, five children and respectability. Had that not been enough?

"Are you all right,. Ma'am?" Cora's concerned voice brought Rose back to the present situation.

"Yes, just lost in thought. Here's the church; let's have a look inside."

She opened the wooden door and again, memories came flooding back, along with the scent of old, faintly damp stone, candlewax and dusty hymnbooks. Rose forced herself to look around, hoping to see Mrs Preston with her bucket. But she and Cora were the only people in the church.

"It'll be ever so nice for your wedding, ma'am," Cora said. "Shame it's winter, 'cause there won't be many flowers, but you could maybe have some evergreen branches or something."

"Yes, evergreens would be attractive. Or possibly my mother knows someone with a hothouse who would have flowers this time of year."

She sighed at the thought of asking; Charlotte would point out the lack of seasonal flowers was yet another reason to delay the wedding until summer or autumn.

Cora twisted her head around, taking in every corner of the church. "That Mrs Preston ain't here, is she? Reckon she's gone back to Miss Appleby's house."

"I believe you're right. Oh, well, it was worth a look."

She turned to leave, and as she did, the door opened. Rose swallowed a yelp of dismay, realizing that if someone had followed her and Cora, meaning them any harm, they would be trapped in the church with little chance of defending themselves. She was just debating how effective a weapon one of the heavy silver candlesticks would be when she identified the person who had come through the door, and relaxed.

"Good heavens, you gave me a start, Miss Appleby," she said. "I didn't expect to see anyone here."

Irene Appleby looked almost as surprised as Rose felt.

"Oh, Mrs Miles," she said. "No, I didn't expect to see anyone here, either."

"Are you a member of this church?" Rose asked, feeling she should take charge of the conversation.

"I attend services on occasion. You will understand I don't want to attract unwanted attention." She glanced at Cora, who was trying to shrink into the background.

"Oh, I see. I don't often come here myself, but Mr Stone and I are going to be married here, so I wanted to look around."

"You weren't looking for me?"

The question surprised Rose. "No, I wasn't. I had no idea this was your church."

"Or perhaps you didn't think that I would attend any church at all, being such a sinful person."

"That is not for me to judge," Rose said. "But since we both are here, may I ask your reason for coming?"

She thought Irene wasn't going to answer, justifiably, since she had no right to ask. But Irene's persistent refusal to say where she had been when Timothy Holt was attacked still rankled.

"To meditate. To pray and seek guidance."

Rose took a chance, hoping that the mystery surrounding Timothy Holt's death was the subject of Irene's meditation or prayer. It seemed likely.

"In that case," she said, "I hope you find it in your heart to provide any information you possess concerning Mr Holt's death to the police. Or if you prefer, to Mr Stone and myself, since I can quite understand your reluctance to deal with the police again."

"Can you? You are respectable, Mrs Miles, and you will be believed if you make a statement. For myself, there would always be a degree of skepticism, even if I were to swear on the Bible I was telling the truth."

"And you feel you cannot confide in me, either?" Rose almost held her breath, because Irene appeared to be considering the possibility.

"No, I'm afraid I can't."

"Not even to help in finding Mr Holt's killer?" She deliberately chose the last word, hoping to jolt Irene into speaking.

To her surprise, Irene smiled at that. A rather rueful smile, but a smile all the same. "Especially not that," she said.

"And you won't say where you were at the time of his death? We know you had a meeting with someone, but you refuse to say who that was."

Irene bowed her head but didn't answer.

"So whatever subject you are seeking spiritual guidance on is something quite different."

"In a way, yes."

It was clear that Irene was not going to say any more and that she wished Rose and Cora would leave her alone. Rose sighed, but felt she should make one last attempt.

"I see you are wearing mourning for Mr Holt, which I can't help feeling is rather daring of you. Almost as if you are making a public announcement, telling people what he meant to you and that you are grieving for your loss."

"How perceptive of you, Mrs Miles," Irene said. "That is precisely why I am wearing it. Now, if you will pardon me, I should like to have some time to myself."

Rose tried to remember if anyone had ever dismissed her so abruptly, and decided they hadn't. There seemed to be nothing left to do but to make a dignified exit, so she said simply, "I hope you find guidance here which will allow you to be more forthcoming than you have been. Come, Cora. Good day, Miss Appleby."

She and Cora left the church and when they were outside, Cora said angrily, "She was right rude to you, ma'am, wasn't she?"

"I think she is under a great deal of mental pressure at the moment," Rose said. "It may have been partly my fault for trying to persuade her to speak of something she is determined not to reveal."

"Oh, I don't think so, ma'am."

Rose smiled at Cora, who was still bristling in her defense. "However, Miss Appleby's desire for solitude does give us the opportunity to call briefly at her house and speak to Mrs Preston. She may not be able to help at all, but then again, she may."

"That's a good idea, ma'am."

Accordingly, instead of turning back toward St Giles, Rose and Cora went the opposite direction, and were soon walking down St John Street. At the door of number 9, Rose lifted the polished knocker and let it fall.

It took a few minutes before there was any response, but then the door opened and a housemaid in a gray dress and crisp white apron looked at them curiously.

"Good morning," Rose said. "I should like a word with Mrs Preston, if she is in."

"The mistress isn't at home, ma'am."

"I know that. I wish to speak to Mrs Preston, not Miss Appleby."

The housemaid looked doubtful, but before she could raise any objection, Mrs Preston appeared behind her.

"Lord help us, it's Mrs Miles," she said. "Ask her to come in, you silly girl."

"But the mistress …"

"It's actually you I wanted to have a brief word with, Mrs Preston," Rose said. "I have just seen Miss Appleby at Holy Trinity Church, so I knew she wouldn't be at home."

"Come inside, do." Mrs Preston elbowed the maid out of the way, leaving a clear space for Rose and Cora to step into the hallway. The maid withdrew into the kitchen, and Mrs Preston lowered her voice. "Is it somethin' important, ma'am? Miss Appleby's name's been cleared, so I know it ain't that."

"No, it's not. Do you know why she was released?"

Mrs Preston wrinkled her forehead. "Thought it were something you and Mr Stone did."

"No. It was because the cab driver who drove Mr Holt on his final trip was stabbed to death yesterday, in exactly the same way as Mr Holt was."

Mrs Preston stared and her jaw dropped slightly, but she said nothing, so Rose continued.

"Since Miss Appleby was in Oxford Prison at the time, she couldn't have been involved, and because the two crimes were so much alike, it was concluded they were carried out by the same person."

"Which weren't her."

"Exactly. Miss Appleby was not told why she had been released, so it came as a shock to her last evening when Mr Stone informed her of the driver's death. What I wanted to ask you, however, was what happened when she returned home yesterday afternoon, before she learned of the second death. I am assuming she was relieved to be at liberty again, but did she do or say anything at all out of the ordinary?"

FOURTEEN

"Let me think," Mrs Preston said. She screwed her eyes shut for a moment and then opened them. "Y'know, we were so glad to see her that I reckon we didn't notice much else."

"I am assuming she was thankful to be free again."

"She was that, to be sure. Looking all round the house like she'd been gone a year, not less than a fortnight. I asked if there was anything I could do for her, and she gave a kind of laugh and said she'd have a bath first thing, change into some clean clothes, and then she'd like a nice cup of tea."

"That sounds reasonable," Rose said, while Cora nodded in agreement.

"So's that what she did. Cook made her a sandwich, bein' as she hadn't had anything to eat, and when she'd had her bath, she had the sandwich and some tea."

"And then what did she do? Did she tell you she was going to my house?"

Mrs Preston twisted her hands together and for the first time in Rose's memory, looked guilty.

"I reckon that was my doing, ma'am. I mean to say, I may have given her the idea of goin'. She was right pleased to be home again but kind of puzzled, sayin' she didn't know why they'd let her go. So I said mebbe Mr Stone knew why, since the coppers hadn't told her."

"I see."

"And she said that was a good idea and that inspector had told her Mr Stone might be at your house and did I know where you lived. So I told her. Reckon I shouldn't have done? I didn't mean no harm by it."

"No, of course you didn't," Rose said. "And no harm was done. It simply meant she found out a bit more quickly about the cab driver's death. She would have learned it sooner or later, you know."

"S'pose so. Did you say she was at the church?"

"Yes, I spoke to her there. Does she attend church services regularly?"

"Not every Sunday, but once in a while." Mrs Preston gave Rose a sly smile. "Reckon she thinks she's broke too many commandments to go regular. You know what them vicars are like, always tryin' to make you feel guilty."

Cora gasped at this criticism of the clergy, but Rose was unmoved.

"I can understand that. Do you know if she's ever gone before just to meditate or pray on her own? Or even to seek advice from the vicar?"

"Don't think so. Not since I've been here, anyway."

Which meant that Irene had something very serious on her mind, to bring her to the church outside of her normal, if erratic, attendance. Rose could only hope it was that she was deciding whether to reveal more about the day Timothy Holt had died, and any information that might help identify his killer. With luck, she might be divinely guided to do so.

But there was no telling how long she might spend in prayer or meditation that morning, and Rose didn't want to be caught questioning her servants, so she said, "And there was nothing else about her return home that caught your attention?"

"Not that I can think of, ma'am."

"Very well, thank you for your help. You know where I live; if you think of anything else, try to get a message to me."

"I'll do my best, ma'am, but I can't write none, so I'd have to get a lad to go and tell you or come meself."

Rose felt mildly guilty for not remembering that someone in Mrs Preston's position would likely never have had the chance to learn to read or write. Cora hadn't either, but over the past few years, Rose had patiently taught her enough that she could read and write simple words. She was quite aware that was not something most employers would do, but her theory was that Cora's literacy would benefit both of them.

"Well, do the best you can. Thank you again."

She started to turn away and Mrs Preston said suddenly, "I've remembered something."

"Yes?"

"Miss Appleby said just before she went to take her bath, 'Mebbe I'll have the chance after all to go ahead with it'. Sort of like she was talkin' to herself. It was you sayin' about sending a message that made me think of it."

"Do you know what she was referring to?"

To Rose's disappointment, Mrs Preston shook her head. "Not for sure, ma'am. But the last time Mr Holt was there, I heard her and him …"

She stopped, and Rose said, "It doesn't matter if you overheard something. I'm sure you weren't deliberately listening to their conversation."

She didn't believe that for a second, but it reassured Mrs Preston.

"She said something about payin' back and about book learnin'. She can read and write and talk with the best of 'em, you know, so I wondered if it were something to do with a school or suchlike."

"That's possible. She told Mr Stone she was a foundling, raised in an orphanage, but she seems to have acquired a fair amount of education somewhere. Did Mr Holt reply?"

"Not that I heard," Mrs Preston said regretfully. "He might have done, but I couldn't stand there with me ears flappin', y'know."

"Of course not. Thank you, Mrs Preston; that could be helpful, even though I don't know exactly how."

She gave her a last smile and turned to go. Once back on the street, she let out a sigh of relief.

"Thank heavens Miss Appleby didn't come back home whilst we were there. That would have been embarrassing, to say the least."

"You would have thought of something to explain why you were there," Cora said loyally.

"I'd like to think so, but I'm not as good at off-the-cuff explanations as Mr Stone is. He can talk his way out of just about any awkward situation."

Theo would have been flattered by that assessment, because at the moment he was facing a situation that was difficult, if not exactly awkward. He had caught the omnibus to Banbury Road, not wanting to waste the time it would have taken to walk, and was now approaching number 77. It was a well-kept brick house, obviously the home of a man with a substantial income, with a neatly swept walk to the front door.

As Theo debated the best angle to take with Gregory Holt, the front door opened and a man came out, walking briskly. He was probably in his forties, wearing a well-tailored black suit, tall, thin and as he came a little closer, Theo could see light eyes under the brim of his hat.

His appearance was so much like that Mrs Preston had given of Timothy Holt that Theo was positive this was

Gregory Holt. So what should he do? He felt that to accost the man on the pavement or follow him down the street would be not only impolite but counterproductive.

Gregory Holt had just lost his brother and undoubtedly had duties to attend to in regard to his death, as well as managing his own business. He wouldn't agree to being interrogated by a nosy investigative agent with no direct interest in his brother's death, and would just brush Theo aside. Especially if that interrogation started in a very public setting.

He gave Theo only an incurious glance as he passed him, his mind obviously on other matters, but Theo could see what Mrs Preston had meant about Timothy Holt's eyes seeming to look right through her. His brother's pale blue eyes were much the same. Theo held a rapid mental debate on whether to say anything or simply let this chance go by and tackle Holt at a better time and place. True, he had now seen the man and could identify him again in a different setting, but would it be advisable to at least introduce himself? A more lengthy conversation could wait.

Banbury Road was a busy thoroughfare, and while Theo was still pondering his options, Gregory held up a hand to hail a passing hansom cab. He spoke to the driver, climbed inside and the cab rolled off.

"Blast it," Theo muttered. "That's what comes of dithering."

He looked around hurriedly and saw an omnibus trundling down the street toward the center of Oxford. It wasn't as good as a cab, but it was faster than walking and would have to do. Theo swung himself on board and took a seat on the outside where he could keep a distant eye on Holt's cab.

However, the omnibus stopped and started as it took on passengers and let others off, and Theo was swearing under his breath as the cab, unhindered by such halts, drew further and further away. By the time the omnibus reached the point where the two roads merged into the wider St Giles, he had lost sight of it altogether.

Dispirited, he disembarked and stood on the pavement, thinking. Gregory Holt had been headed into the center of town, probably to conduct some business transaction or visit a company he had funded. He would go home at some point, but Theo could hardly loiter outside, possibly for hours, waiting for him to return. The only consolation he could see at the moment was that Caldwell had given him the correct address to find the man.

He imagined Rose would have gone to Holy Trinity by now, so Theo decided to head in that direction, thinking he might intercept her and they could walk back together. If she had been lucky enough to locate Mrs Preston, she might have some new information to share.

Accordingly, he lengthened his stride and soon turned into the street where the church was. An hansom cab passed him as he walked, but he paid no attention to it. And then he stopped abruptly, because the cab was drawing away, but there on the pavement, not fifty yards from him, was Gregory Holt.

Now what, Theo asked himself, was Holt doing there? He seemed to be bound for the church, pausing outside its door and looking around. Theo bent over as if to pick up a dropped glove or coin, and when he straightened up, Holt had gone inside, the wooden door closing behind him.

Theo wondered whether Rose was also in the church, and after a few moments, decided she wasn't. He based this on the theory that even if she had found Mrs Preston, she wouldn't continue a conversation with Gregory Holt present, and would promptly leave. There was no reason to think he had stabbed both his brother and a cab driver to death, but common sense told Theo that Gregory was the one man who could have got close to Timothy Holt without arousing suspicion.

So he stood on the street corner, occasionally glancing at his pocket watch as if waiting for someone. That wasn't entirely a fabrication, since he thought Rose might be somewhere around. Ten minutes had passed before the church door opened again, and Holt came out.

Again he looked around and saw only Theo, studying his watch with the impatient air of a man waiting for a friend to appear. He walked away in the direction of the town center and after letting him get a street ahead, Theo strolled after him.

Rose took her coat and hat off and went into the drawing room to review the information she had learned from her excursion. It wasn't very much, she had to admit. About the only new elements were that Irene Appleby had gone to the church to think over a serious issue, and that she might have some interest in a school or other form of education.

Neither of those items did anything, as far as she could see, to get them any closer to learning who had killed Timothy Holt, and then, a fortnight later, killed the man who had driven him on his last ride. That was an intriguing question – why had they waited so long? And of course, there was no way of knowing why they considered Bellamy a threat.

"D'ye want a cup of tea, ma'am?" Cora was hovering in the doorway, obviously reluctant to interrupt Rose's train of thought.

"Yes, please. Cora, tell me something."

"Yes, ma'am?"

"What do you think about Miss Appleby wearing mourning for a man she was not related to? She indicated she was doing so deliberately."

"I s'pose she *is* mourning, in a way," Cora said cautiously. She knew better than anyone how Rose had felt imprisoned in her mandatory head-to-toe black clothing after Edward's death, and why it puzzled her that Irene would wear mourning when she didn't have to.

"Yes, I suppose so. But to deliberately invite comment … one wonders."

"If anyone asked, she could say it was for some relation. If she was brought up in an orphanage, no one would know any different."

"That's a thought. Perhaps that is what she intends to do."

Cora beamed at the praise. "I'll get the tea, now, ma'am."

She went off to the kitchen and Rose continued her musing. She hoped Theo had been able to speak to Holt's solicitor and perhaps also to his brother. He would have to be both tactful and persuasive to extract information, but she had great confidence in him.

Of somewhat more interest was why Irene had been so curious about the reason behind her release that she couldn't bear to wait even a day to speak to Theo and Rose. It almost argued that she had a theory about it, and that theory had nothing to do with William Bellamy. Her shock on hearing of his murder had been genuine, Rose was certain. So what explanation had she expected to be given?

She was still pondering Irene's behavior when Theo arrived an hour later, sinking into an armchair with a sigh of relief.

"I feel as if I have walked to London and back," he said. "My feet and I have not been on speaking terms for at least half an hour."

Rose handed him a cup of tea. "Could you not have taken a cab? Or have you lost the taste for that mode of transport?"

"It's not that. If one is following someone who is on foot, one is obliged to do the same. Cab drivers don't like being told that their passenger has no idea where he may be going."

"Ah, I see. Who were you following?"

145

"Gregory Holt. I first went to see the solicitor, Mr Caldwell, who was as helpful as he could be without breaching confidences. Basically, he said that Miss Appleby was not mentioned in Timothy Holt's will, but that he had already made ample provision for her, and she was aware of that."

"Provision as in investments, something of that sort?"

"I imagine so."

"That's interesting, Theo, because I received a hint from Mrs Preston that she might be involved in funding a school of some sort. I suppose she could use the money however she wished."

"Unless there was some sort of caveat, yes. And it is still more confirmation that she didn't stab him, not that we believe she did. His death would not have benefitted her financially, and she knew that. This tea is saving my life, Rose. Is there more in the pot?"

Rose refilled his cup. He drank half of it in one long gulp, and then continued.

"After seeing Mr Caldwell, who supplied me with Gregory Holt's address, I went to find Mr Holt. He lives a fair way out Banbury Road, and I didn't walk there. I took the omnibus. I was debating how to approach him when he came out of his front door, brushed past me and hailed a cab."

"How thoughtless of him."

"Well, yes. It did rather take me by surprise, and I felt chasing after him would be neither dignified nor prudent. My only means of available transport was another omnibus, but I couldn't catch up with the cab."

"So you weren't able to speak to him. Never mind. There will be other opportunities."

"Ah, but wait. I didn't lose him altogether. I thought I might find you at Holy Trinity, so I went there, only to see Mr Holt ahead of me. That was a piece of luck, to be sure. He went into the church, stayed for some ten minutes, and then left to set off on foot toward the center of town. I followed him … Rose, what is it?"

Rose was staring at him, her dark blue eyes wide. "When did you see Mr Holt go into the church?" she asked. "I mean to say, approximately what time was it? Do you remember?"

"I would have said about half ten, or perhaps a little later. I was standing on the next street corner, pretending to be waiting for someone and looking at my watch frequently, so I am reasonably sure of the time. Why?"

"Because shortly before that, Cora and I went to the church to look for Mrs Preston, and Miss Appleby came in. She almost chased us out, saying she wanted to be alone to meditate. But given the time we left and the time you saw Mr Holt arrive, it seems much more likely she had a pre-arranged meeting with him and didn't want anyone – especially you or I – to know about it. It's no wonder she was so eager that we should leave, if she was expecting him to appear."

FIFTEEN

"Now that is very interesting indeed," Theo said. "It's not inconceivable that she may have met Gregory Holt at some point, but why the secretive meeting today?"

"I've no idea. You don't suppose she was transferring her allegiance from one brother to the other, do you?"

"I hope not. I admit she hasn't been totally honest with us, but that would indicate a disappointing level of duplicity."

"That's a polite way of putting it," Rose said. "It could be, I suppose, that she simply wanted to speak to him without anyone else listening. I don't know if Gregory Holt is married, but if he is, his wife might not take kindly to an attractive young woman appearing on the doorstep requesting a private conversation with him."

"Even though the subject of that conversation could well be simply a financial one. I take it you did manage to see Mrs Preston?"

"Yes, at Miss Appleby's house. I assumed because she was at the church, I could call there safely."

"You have the instincts of a good detective," Theo said gravely. "People cannot be in two places at once, a fact which has worked to Miss Appleby's advantage. What did Mrs Preston tell you?"

Rose recounted her conversation with Mrs Preston. "The only element of interest is that mention of something such as a school. Could she have been planning to invest money in one?"

"Possibly. If I can speak to Gregory Holt, he may be kind enough to tell me. That may even have been what the two of them were discussing at Holy Trinity. But I can't see for the life of me why her potential investment in a school should lead to the murder of her benefactor."

"Nor can I. I told Cook you would probably be having lunch here, so shall we have something to eat whilst we decide what to do next?"

Over the omelette, salad and cheese, Theo finished the sentence which had been abandoned by the discovery that Irene Appleby and Gregory Holt had met secretly in the church.

"I followed Mr Holt into town, and I must say, he is a very energetic man. He called at two small businesses, although I can't say whether he was there as a customer or because he had invested in them. Then he went to Mr Caldwell's chambers, so it was just as well I had already been there. It would have been a bit awkward if we had arrived at the same time."

"It would indeed."

"He didn't remain long, so it can't have been a very serious matter which took him there. Perhaps something to do with his brother's will."

"Do you think Mr Caldwell will have told him you called earlier?"

Theo paused with his fork in mid-air. "I certainly hope not, although I couldn't very well swear him to secrecy. He'd have no reason to mention me, and considering that he was rather secretive about the way he provided Gregory's address ... no, I don't think so. I did leave a card in case he wanted to contact us about anything."

"We don't know if Gregory Holt was on the same terms with Mr Caldwell as his brother was, do we? However, we have to assume that as his friend and his brother, Mr Caldwell and Gregory Holt have a mutual interest in finding out who murdered him."

"Unless one of them did it. I was thinking that Timothy Holt would have no reason to be on his guard if his brother or friend approached him in Beaumont Street."

Rose considered this. Theo had a point, but hadn't the police determined that Gregory Holt had been in Banbury that day? She didn't know if the solicitor's whereabouts had been investigated, but what motive would Caldwell have to kill a man who was both a client and a friend?

Neither of them would benefit financially, and it seemed just as doubtful that Irene would transfer her affections to her benefactor's murderer.

"I can't see it, Theo. Besides, the police said Gregory Holt was in Banbury that day. Not Banbury Road, but the town itself, however many miles away it is."

"True. And according to Sergeant Bennett, they have witnesses to prove that."

"So we shall dismiss Gregory Holt as a potential assassin. Where did he go after his visit to the solicitor?"

"He trotted down the High toward St Clements."

"Not another assignation in a church, I hope."

"No. I followed him all the way to Stockmore Street, where, you will remember, Timothy Holt lived with his family. He was obviously paying them – or at least his sister-in-law – a visit. I couldn't say what the purpose was. Possibly to advise on some financial aspect, or merely to see how they were faring."

Rose's mind went back to the days following Edward's death. She had received very few callers, probably because no one was quite sure what to say to her. Her own sisters had admitted feeling awkward and unsure, worried that they would say the wrong thing and upset her. Frankly, Rose had been so shocked by her unexpected widowhood that nothing would have had much impact, but she had still felt somewhat neglected. She wondered if Georgia Holt felt the same.

"That was considerate of him."

"You wouldn't say that if you had walked the length and breadth of Oxford following him, only to have him leave there after just a few minutes and start back into town. I tell you, Rose, this is a man who does not waste time in pleasantries, and in fact, does not waste time at all. In and out of Holy Trinity, in and out of two businesses, in and out of Caldwell's chambers and then in and out of his late brother's house, all before lunch. I was quite exhausted."

Rose gave him a sympathetic smile. She knew that in reality, he was proud of successfully following Gregory around Oxford, even though only his meeting with Irene was of real interest. The rest could be easily explained.

"Well, you shan't have to walk anywhere this afternoon, as far as I know. Where did you leave Mr Holt?"

"He walked all the way to Carfax, where he hailed another hansom cab. By this time, I had succeeded in getting close enough to hear him speak to the driver and give him the Banbury Road address. I imagine he was going home for a meal, and since I saw no point in following him further, I came here."

"Let us hope he arrived at his home without being stabbed," Rose said. "Taking a cab ride seems to be fraught with danger for anyone associated with Timothy Holt."

Theo stared at her for a moment, thinking how disastrous it would be if the murderer claimed a third victim. There was no reason to think Gregory Holt wouldn't have arrived safely at his destination, but still …

"I saw no one any closer to him than I was," he said, "and he boarded the cab with no indication that someone had attacked him. I tell you, Rose, I shall be on tenterhooks until someone – either us or the police – identifies Timothy Holt and William Bellamy's killer."

Theo left for Willows after lunch, having first gone to his rented rooms and discovering a terse note from his publisher wanting to know how soon the manuscript of *Honesty for Sale* might be delivered to him. It was coming along nicely, Theo felt, but he was aware that the events of the past few days had kept him away from his writing desk more than usual.

He composed a return letter assuring the publisher that the novel was in the final stages of completion, and posted it without feeling very guilty. Half an hour later he was writing feverishly, having got to the point where the murderer was about to be dramatically revealed.

Theo paused, flexed his cramped fingers and wished real life would be so accommodating. It was still hard to believe that two men could have been fatally stabbed without anyone noticing anything amiss. That argued the killer had been either someone that both Holt and Bellamy had trusted, or someone so insignificant that they had been overlooked.

In the first instance, there would appear to be no way the two men would have occupied the same social circle, and were unlikely to have mutual acquaintances. So how had they been connected? Was it simply that Bellamy had driven Holt to or from his assignations more than once? Mrs Preston didn't think he always used the same driver, so it appeared Bellamy had just been extremely unlucky.

As for the possibility of an insignificant person being the assassin, Theo shook his head. There were so many people who could have passed by without being noticed that it would be impossible to identify any one in particular.

In the room next to where he was writing, workmen were replacing the tiles above the kitchen worktops, since several had been cracked or chipped, and Rose hadn't liked them much anyway. So she had chosen new ones, and the workmen were taking the old ones off before installing their replacements. The process was not a silent one, but Theo had discovered once he got into his writing, it took a great deal to distract him.

So the crack and clatter of ceramic tiles being broken up and thrown into a bin for removal barely registered, until a particularly loud crash made him pause and look up. And that led to another thought – had someone created a distraction that had allowed Holt's killer to get close enough to stab him while his attention was elsewhere?

That would mean two people were involved, but that was not an insurmountable problem. It would have been easy enough to recruit some street urchin to bang dustbin lids, throw stones to break a window or simply start shouting nearby. Holt would naturally have turned to look at the scene of the disturbance, and a few seconds was all his attacker needed.

Then they would have melted into the stream of pedestrians and Holt might not have realized how badly wounded he was until it was too late. A variation of the same technique could have been used on Bellamy, who had been stabbed on an even busier street.

Feeling that he might have come up with a viable theory, Theo jotted down a note, so he wouldn't forget to mention it to Rose when he saw her later. He went back to his manuscript, and was shortly immersed in the problem of deciding the villain's fate, since the reading public demanded that a price be paid for his crimes.

The fictional villain had just been marched off by the constabulary when Theo became aware that someone was hammering on the front door. He pushed his chair back and went to open it, finding a young boy on the walk holding a note.

"Yes?"

"You Mr Stone?"

"Yes."

"This here's for you." The boy handed Theo the paper, and hovered, awaiting a reply, a tip, or both. Theo opened the paper and read:

"Gregory Holt has called. Are you able to come here? Rose."

Theo's eyebrows rose. "Run back to number 21 and tell Mrs Miles I will be there very shortly. Here." He handed the boy sixpence and watched him race off down the street.

What could Gregory Holt want with the Milestone Agency, Theo asked himself. He'd obviously been told they were involved, either by Irene Appleby or Bernard Caldwell, and most likely wanted to find out if they possessed any information the police lacked. Conversely, it was possible Holt wanted to advise them to drop their investigation now that Irene had been cleared of suspicion.

Theo remembered that Rose had suggested that possibility and he had argued for continuing. With a feeling of mild guilt, he put his hat and coat on, told the workmen he would be out for a while, and started toward Rose's house.

Rose had been astonished when Pickett told her who was at the door, and for a moment she considered telling him she was not at home. She fingered Holt's engraved calling card, wondering what he could want. Information? Delivering a stern warning to leave well enough alone? Or just possibly, asking them to continue investigating his brother's death?

"If you will ask him to wait for a moment, I need to have a message sent to Mr Stone at Willows."

"Yes, ma'am." Pickett's face showed he approved of this action. Mrs Miles, however respectable, should not be entertaining strange men without her husband-to-be at least being aware of it.

He returned to the hallway while Rose wrote a brief note. She knew as soon as Holt was inside the drawing room, Pickett would find a boy to deliver the message, and she only hoped Theo was not in the midst of a crucial plot element when he received it.

The drawing room door opened and Rose composed herself.

"Mr Gregory Holt, ma'am."

"Good afternoon, Mr Holt," she said. "I'm Rose Miles. Do have a chair, please. I regret that Mr Stone is not here just now, since I assume you wish to speak with us both, but I have sent him a message and he should be here shortly."

Holt seated himself, tucking his coat tails neatly behind him and placing his hat on the floor beside the chair. Rose sat down opposite him.

"Thank you, Mrs Miles," he said. "You are quite correct;, I would prefer to speak to both of you, if only because I feel Mr Stone deserves some compensation for his efforts in following me around Oxford this morning."

There was not much Rose could say to that, and she only hoped Theo wouldn't be too disappointed to learn he had been seen. She hastened to smooth over the situation.

"Mr Stone had hoped to call on you at your home, but you were just leaving as he arrived and he felt he shouldn't interfere with your planned schedule. You are, according to him, a very busy man."

She smiled as warmly as she could manage, noting that like his brother, Gregory had pale blue eyes that were rather hard to meet. She was also determined not to mention the meeting with Irene, preferring to hold that back. Further conversation might reveal whether Holt knew Theo had seen him at the church.

"Yes, I am. I neither boast of it nor apologize. And in case you are wondering how I identified him, he first came to my attention as I arrived at my solicitor's chambers. I mentioned to Mr Caldwell that a young man seemed to be dogging my footsteps, and he rather reluctantly said that might be Mr Theodore Stone, who had called on him previously. A physical description confirmed the fact. The card he left provided this address."

Holt smiled unexpectedly, and Rose hoped that meant he wasn't too angry.

"He patronizes a decent tailor, I noted. Much better than being shadowed, I believe the term is, by some scruffy ne'er do well."

"Mr Stone will be pleased to hear you approve of his appearance, as will his tailor," Rose said, relaxing a little. "But I doubt you came here to comment on his wardrobe. Is your visit to do with your brother's untimely death?"

"Of course it is."

"Then may I offer you some refreshment whilst we wait for Mr Stone to arrive? A cup of tea, perhaps?"

"Thank you."

Rose rang for Cora and ordered tea for three, assuming Theo would join them shortly. Holt looked around the comfortable drawing room, which Rose had to admit, did not resemble what the premises of an investigative agency might be expected to look like. She wondered how much Theo had told Caldwell about the Milestone Agency and how much had been passed on to Holt.

Cora came with the tea and as Rose poured it out, she heard Theo arriving. She hoped her sigh of relief wasn't audible as he came in, and hastened to make the introductions.

"Mr Stone, Mr Gregory Holt. He is here in connection with his brother's death."

Theo noted that she hadn't specified the connection and offered a hand to Holt.

"I am pleased to make your acquaintance, Mr Holt," he said. "I hope we can be of service to you."

"Likewise, Mr Stone. Our previous 'acquaintance', as one might term it, was from a distance as you followed me through Oxford."

If Theo was disconcerted, he didn't show it. "I obviously was not as discreet as I had hoped to be. Never mind, practice makes perfect, as they say. As a matter of interest, when did you first notice me?"

"In Queen Street, shortly before I went to call on Mr Caldwell."

Which meant he wasn't aware Theo had seen him going to Holy Trinity church or that Rose had seen Irene there. Theo cleared his throat.

"May I ask you a preliminary question, Mr Holt?"

"Yes."

"Since you are here about your brother's death, you are no doubt aware of Miss Irene Appleby's role in his life and that she was held – and subsequently released – on suspicion of being involved in his death. One reason she was suspected was that she could provide no firm alibi for her whereabouts at the time he was attacked. Subsequently, she said she had gone to meet someone, but refused to say who that was, or where the meeting took place.

"We have been told you were in Banbury that day. So I'd have to ask – to clear up that detail – do you have any idea who it was that Miss Appleby went to meet with?"

SIXTEEN

Holt's pale blue eyes bored into Theo, who was sure that he knew the answer and equally sure that he wasn't going to reveal it. Holt's next words confirmed that.

"I can understand why you want to know this, Mr Stone, but I see no reason why I should tell you. Unlike the police, you have no official standing and cannot compel me to disclose information."

"Absolutely. That is understood. What I don't understand, however, is why that meeting, if innocent, is so shrouded in secrecy. First, Miss Appleby refused to give any details, and now you, if I'm not mistaken, are also going to refuse."

"I regret to say that is so. If Miss Appleby wishes to divulge the information, that is her decision. As you say, she has now been cleared of any suspicion in Timothy's death, so it hardly matters."

"It matters," Rose said, "because it appears she is trying to shield someone. Presumably that isn't yourself."

"No. As you know, I was not even in Oxford that day."

"And you refuse to tell us, even though it is obvious you know who she met."

Holt smiled again. "Not even to oblige a lady as charming as yourself, Mrs Miles."

"So why are you here, Mr Holt?" Theo asked. "It would not appear to be to champion Miss Appleby, since she does not need your protection from criminal charges."

"You may attribute it to curiosity. You spent some time following me around Oxford, so I assume you wished to speak to me. I'd like to know why. Here I am; speak to me."

Theo and Rose exchanged glances, silently debating who should take the lead. Rose nodded.

"We have met Miss Appleby," she said. "Having done so, we could understand your brother's interest in her. She is not only very attractive, but intelligent as well, don't you think?"

"I would say …" Holt stopped. "Cleverly done, Mrs Miles. Yes, I have met Miss Appleby and agree with your assessment. No doubt that is what you wanted me to confess. However, if you were thinking I would try and lure her away from Timothy, you are quite mistaken. I don't poach on another man's territory, and particularly not my brother's."

"You were close to him." Rose made it a statement.

"Yes." A shadow passed across Holt's face and Rose felt a little guilty about mentioning his bereavement, but not guilty enough to keep from questioning him further.

"And now, you may feel a responsibility toward his widow and children."

"Yes. As a matter of fact, I saw my sister-in-law today."

Rose tried to pretend this wasn't news to her. Holt probably wouldn't know that Theo was aware of why he had gone to Stockmore Street.

"I am sure she was pleased to see you. I know how isolated one feels whilst in mourning."

She caught Holt's glance at her black dress and said, "I am a widow, too, Mr Holt. She must appreciate your support at this time. May I ask – do you also feel any responsibility toward Irene Appleby?"

Holt didn't answer immediately, probably trying to determine where the questions might be leading.

"I would not call it a responsibility," he said finally. "Timothy provided her with enough funds that, sensibly invested, she need not have any financial worries for years to come. If she wishes to consult me on those matters, I would be willing to advise her."

"Yes, we understand you and your brother make a practice of providing both funds and financial advice," Theo said. "Was that the purpose of your meeting with Miss Appleby this morning?"

For a moment, both Theo and Rose thought Holt was going to simply stand up and walk out of the room. He actually rose an inch or so from his chair, then sat back down again.

"I may have underestimated you, Mr Stone," he said.

"So you are not going to deny that you met with her?"

"No, since you obviously know that I did."

"And will you tell us what you spoke of?"

"Largely concerning financial matters. She wished to consult me in confidence."

"Were the financial matters so secret?" Rose asked.

"Confidentiality is not the same as secrecy, Mrs Miles."

"No, of course not. In your conversation, did she mention a school at all?"

There was no mistaking Holt's surprise at that question. His eyebrows went up and his hands tightened on the arms of the chair.

"A school?"

"Or an educational institution of some sort."

They waited while Holt considered his response. Had he immediately denied any conversation concerning a school, they would have had one answer. Since he hadn't, Rose's question had apparently hit its mark.

"Yes, she did," he said. "It is something she wishes to do, and I am willing to help her, as was Timothy. I am not certain how practical it would be, but as you may have gathered, she is rather determined."

"What sort of school would it be?" Theo asked.

"A small one, for children who otherwise would have no chance to learn to read and write and do basic arithmetic. Perhaps a bit of history and geography. Nothing elaborate. She was given some schooling at the orphanage where she spent several years, and she has always been grateful for that."

"So she wishes to benefit other children in the same manner," Rose said. "That sounds a very generous and worthy cause. Why should it be a secret?"

"Because she wishes to remain anonymous. You will understand, I hope, that society frowns on her association with Timothy, and the idea of a successful man's mistress using money he provided to her to educate children who are generally not felt to need education – well, you can see why she is not eager that her name be associated with it. And Timothy himself wished to remain one step removed."

"Yes, I see," Rose said. "A worthy cause, all the same."

"I'm delighted that you approve," Holt said drily.

"So I hope you will be able to advise her wisely," Theo said. "During your conversation this morning, did Miss Appleby tell you why the police released her without charge?"

"No, she did not. Does it matter? Presumably the police found some evidence pointing to someone else, enough to make them realize she was not involved."

Again, Theo and Rose looked at each other, and this time it was Theo who spoke first.

"I presume you know the circumstances of your brother's death?"

"Yes. Inspector Reed told me what the police believe happened."

"And when you spoke to Miss Appleby, she did not tell you about William Bellamy?"

"No. Who is he? Someone who may have attacked Timothy?"

"William Bellamy," Theo said, "is the driver who took your brother on his final journey. And he was stabbed to death in much the same manner yesterday afternoon."

Holt's reaction was to sit extremely still, his face suddenly looking as though it was carved from stone. He said nothing for a full minute, as if thinking over Theo's blunt statement.

Finally he said, "Have the police confirmed that?"

"Yes."

"So they are assuming the same person was responsible for both murders."

"Yes."

Holt didn't need to have the corollary spelled out for him. He said promptly, "And that it was not Miss Appleby."

"No. She was in prison at the time of Bellamy's death."

"What steps have the police taken to identify the actual criminal?"

"You understand," Theo said, "Inspector Reed does not confide every detail of his investigations to us, even when we are involved. So I can't say, except that naturally he and his men would be interviewing anyone who might either have witnessed any suspicious activity, or anyone who might know of a reason why your brother should have been attacked."

Holt nodded. "Yes, he spoke to me the day Timothy died. He asked if I knew of anyone with a reason to want him dead. It was not very tactful, but I expect tact takes second place to expediency in matters of this sort."

"What did you tell the inspector?" Rose asked. "Did your brother have enemies?"

"Not that I am aware of. He was respected, even liked, by a great number of people."

"How about business rivals?" Theo asked.

Holt smiled, as if deploring Theo's naiveté. "We do not run businesses, Mr Stone. We simply supply funds to make them possible. Therefore, we don't have competitors, or rivals, as such. The risk is all our own. If the business succeeds, we share in the success. If not, we absorb the loss."

He sat back, crossing one elegantly clad leg over the other. "It's not like your family's business, where you constantly have to be out-thinking and out-producing other breweries."

It was Theo's turn to be momentarily disconcerted. But then he found himself chuckling.

"I congratulate you, Mr Holt. You must have been doing some very rapid research to discover my family background so quickly."

"Not that rapid," Holt said. "Your parents, as I understand it, live not far from my brother's family. Gossip being what it is, some time ago my sister-in-law relayed to my wife the shocking fact that a family whose income derived from brewing beer lived nearby. Worse, your mother appeared to be entirely respectable."

"Oh, she is."

"And that your parents had four sons, the eldest named Theodore, and it seems he was spurning the family business in order to pursue some rather dubious activities."

Theo was laughing openly now. "I should have known. Yes, I write sensational novels which sell quite well, and Mrs Miles and I undertake investigations when requested."

"And who, may I ask, requested your participation in this matter?"

Holt's voice sharpened on that question, much as Theo imagined it would if he were speaking to a business owner who was losing money. He saw no reason not be truthful.

"One of her servants, whom we had met before, asked us to look into it. She was very concerned."

"I see. Miss Appleby has a gift of inspiring devotion. Still, if I have understood you, the actual event which freed her was the death of this unfortunate cab driver."

"I'm afraid so. I had spoken to her, but can't take credit for her release."

"Why are you still involved, then?"

Before Theo could answer, Rose said politely, "Are you requesting that we *not* be involved, Mr Holt? That we leave the entire investigation to the police, who have many other crimes to deal with?"

Holt was visibly torn. Theo thought he would probably prefer to tell them to cease any investigation and leave it to the police, but on the other hand, he might realize the Milestone duo could be more successful than an overworked police force in finding his brother's killer.

He was also thinking that Holt was still holding back useful facts, the main one being who Irene Appleby had been meeting when her benefactor was killed. There seemed no good reason for that, unless, as they had surmised with Irene, he was protecting someone.

Had the police been hoodwinked, and Gregory had not been in Banbury that day? Witnesses could lie, or simply be mistaken. But why would he stab a brother he appeared to have been close to?

"I would appreciate it," Holt said finally, "if you would suspend your efforts. The police may be more competent than you think. At the very least, Mr Stone, please stop following me about Oxford. I assure you that my movements are not very interesting and have nothing to do with Timothy's death."

"They may not be," Theo said, "but I can't promise that we will drop it altogether, and I shouldn't think you would want us to. We don't expect you to pay us, incidentally."

"In that case, I am thankful you aren't asking me to invest in your agency," Holt said. "Working without remuneration is never a good idea, although I suppose your writing is a secondary source of income. We seem to be at an impasse, Mr Stone. You wish to continue your investigation, for no good reason that I can see, and I wish you to abandon it, or at least suspend it."

"Also for no good reason?" Rose inquired politely.

"None that I care to share with you, Mrs Miles. Let us simply say that my family has suffered a great loss and the less upheaval made about it, the better. The police are investigating; let them do their job."

"Very well," Rose said, somewhat to Theo's surprise. It was not like her to capitulate so easily. But then she restored his faith in her. "May I ask you one final question, Mr Holt?"

Holt could not refuse without sounding rude, and he said, "If you must."

"Did your brother's wife know about his relationship with Miss Appleby?"

Gregory Holt had been reasonably amiable until that point, almost as if he was enjoying a verbal sparring session. Rose's question, however, made him clench his jaw and frown, and Theo was sure that if he rather than Rose had asked it, he would have found himself invited outside to settle the matter physically.

"I see no reason for you to ask that question or for me to answer it," he said.

"Oh, come now," Theo said. "It is a simple, obvious question, and I am sure you know the answer. If you refuse to say, we will assume Mrs Holt was well aware of the relationship, although we will have to guess at her reaction."

Holt looked from one to the other. "Yes, she knew," he said through gritted teeth. "Naturally, she disapproved, but a well-bred lady does not air her personal grievances in public."

"Thank you," Rose said. "We assumed as much, but it is well to have confirmation."

Holt stood up. "I shall leave before you decide to ask any other impertinent questions," he said. "And I will ask again that you leave the investigation into Timothy's death – and that of the cab driver – to the police. Good day."

He got to the door so quickly that Pickett barely had time to open it for him. When the front door had closed behind him, Theo looked at Rose.

"That was rather illuminating, wasn't it?"

"It was indeed. A second person close to Timothy Holt asking us to leave the investigation to the police. That argues that there is something both of them know about his death that they are hiding and assuming the police will not uncover."

"I fully agree. However, we do now know that Georgia Holt knew of the relationship. We'll take it for granted that the knowledge created a negative emotion in her, whether that was anger, jealousy, resentment, humiliation or … something else."

"It would also be interesting to know when she learned of it," Rose said, "whether it was fairly recent, or some time ago. From what Mrs Preston said, it was hardly a new arrangement, and it seems to have been common knowledge amongst the ladies of the neighborhood."

"No. On the day he died, Timothy Holt told Miss Appleby he might not be able to see her for a while. I wonder if that was to distance himself from the proposed school, or a more personal reason."

"Such as his wife becoming more vocal about her feelings?"

"That could be," Theo said. "Or someone threatening to make his relationship with Miss Appleby public knowledge."

"Would he have cared about that?" In Rose's world, men were allowed to do more or less as they pleased, providing they were reasonably discreet. As long as Timothy Holt behaved himself in a public setting and provided for his family, his private activities would be ignored or glossed over.

"I don't know. We have the disadvantage of not ever having met him, and neither Miss Appleby nor his brother can be considered unbiased sources."

"True enough. I suppose you want to return to your writing, Theo. These unexpected callers may be interesting, but not helping you finish your book. And to be honest, they don't seem to be getting us much further forward."

"So you are saying politely that we should do as asked, and not pursue it?"

"I'm not sure."

They sat in silence for a moment and then Theo said, "I think rather than writing, I shall go to the police station and have a word with Inspector Reed, if I can. I have the impression that we are missing a crucial piece of the puzzle, and perhaps the police are in possession of it. Contributing our findings – as I promised the inspector we would do – might be helpful."

"Certainly, if you wish. And at some point, we might call on your mother again, to see if she has heard anything about the Holt family – Mrs Holt in particular – and how they are faring. I found that remark of Mrs Minton's intriguing, that Mrs Holt was having difficulty paying household expenses. Surely she must be able to secure credit if she is not able to immediately withdraw cash."

Theo looked at her questioningly and she added, "That is what I had to do after Edward's death, since everything was in his name. It took a while for it to be transferred to me, even though he had made a will when we were first married, specifying that in the event of his death, if there were no children, his assets would come to me."

"Interesting," Theo said. "Very sensible, of course. I wonder what the financial situation is in the Holt family. There are children, but none of them are of age yet, so I would assume Mrs Holt would be the beneficiary. That was the impression Mr Caldwell gave."

"And since money, or the expectation of it, is the motive behind many murders ..."

"Exactly."

SEVENTEEN

Rose saw Theo leave for the police station with some misgivings, since she had no assurance some other person connected to Timothy Holt wouldn't turn up on her doorstep. However, she admitted it would be useful to know if the police had made any more progress.

Useful to whom? she scolded herself. *We have now been asked to back away by both the first victim's brother and his mistress, and it can't be because either of them can be considered suspects. I wouldn't be surprised to find someone representing William Bellamy turning up to demand the same thing.*

She didn't like to think that Georgia Holt would have knifed her husband and an innocent cab driver to death, and even as Rose considered the possibility, a snag appeared. Georgia might have attacked Timothy Holt in Beaumont Street as he returned from a visit to his mistress, but as Rose knew all too well, a recent widow would have been a virtual prisoner in her home for months after her husband's death. She could hardly have been lurking in Carfax a fortnight later, waiting for an opportunity to stab William Bellamy.

That wasn't the only obstacle. No wife of Georgia Holt's class would ever admit to being humiliated or angry if her husband took a mistress. She might be seething inside, but no emotion would be displayed in public.

But then Rose paused, as another thought struck her.

Being forced to stifle her emotions in that manner might make Georgia twice as dangerous. What if for some reason she suddenly snapped and decided her husband should pay for his infidelity? After all, divorce was out of the question, leaving her only one way of ending the marriage.

What am I saying? Rose asked herself. *That a respectable wife and mother took a knife and crept up on her husband in a public place, intending to kill him? And then did the same to an innocent cab driver whilst she was in the first few days of mourning?*

It seemed so impossible that she shook her head. The only scenario she could see where that would happen would be if Timothy Holt had done something absolutely unforgiveable, such as announcing he was planning to leave the family home and live with Irene Appleby. Since neither Irene nor Gregory Holt had given any hint that was what he was planning, she discarded the idea.

If revenge or punishment was not the motive, then what was? She and Theo had mentioned money as prompting many a murder, but it was hard to see how Georgia Holt would be any better off with her husband dead than she would be with him alive and bringing a substantial income to the household. Another idea to be discarded, unless Timothy Holt's solicitor was lying about the terms of his will.

But if he wasn't, why was his widow having such trouble with finances? Rose remembered that even in the first confused days after Edward's death, she had forced herself to deal with household accounts and make sure bills and the servants' wages were paid. In fact, she had almost welcomed the responsibility as a distraction.

The more Rose thought about it, the more puzzled she became. She could only hope Theo was having more luck at the police station, because if not, they might be forced to abandon the case simply for lack of progress.

Theo had been fortunate enough to catch Inspector Reed not only in his office but in a relatively cooperative mood, probably because he was as frustrated as Theo and Rose at not making any headway in solving the two murders.

Theo was not about to quibble, however, and accepted Reed's invitation to sit down and share any information he happened to possess. He was even offered a cup of tea, proof that Reed was growing desperate.

"Mrs Miles and I had an unexpected visit this afternoon from Timothy Holt's brother," Theo said, wrapping his hands around the hot cup. "Much of what passed there will not be news to you, but there were two small items that may be. One, he had a meeting with Miss Appleby this morning which he was at pains to conceal. Two, he said they were discussing, amongst other things, Miss Appleby's proposal to establish a small school for poor children. Timothy Holt's money would have helped provide funding and I suppose she hoped Gregory Holt would also contribute."

As expected, Reed dismissed the prospective school as irrelevant and asked, "How do you know he wanted to conceal the meeting with Miss Appleby?"

Theo explained briefly about Irene chasing Rose and Cora from the church and then his own sighting of Gregory Holt shortly afterwards.

"I have to admit that was accidental, but fortuitous. Faced with no alternative, he admitted meeting with her."

"I see." Reed scribbled a note and then looked up. "How did he know who you were, in order to call on Mrs Miles and yourself later?"

Theo sighed. "Because I had already called on Bernard Caldwell, the Holt brothers' solicitor, and left a card with him. I am not as adept at following people unnoticed as I would like to think and Mr Holt saw me when I followed him to Mr Caldwell's chambers. He described me and Mr Caldwell told him my name and address."

Reed's mouth twitched in a smile. "That is what comes of amateurs meddling in official matters, Mr Stone."

"I hope you aren't going to warn us off, too," Theo said. "We've already been advised by both Miss Appleby and Mr Holt that our assistance is not needed."

"How humiliating for you. No, I shan't warn you off, in the event you stumble across some helpful piece of evidence. Do you have any other information that might prove useful? To the police, that is?"

"Only that we have learned Mrs Holt appears to be having some financial difficulties. I've no idea why. Mr Caldwell said her husband's will was straightforward enough, providing for her and the children. Of course, one woman's serious difficulties may be another's minor inconvenience. May I ask you a question, Inspector?"

"Yes."

"Did you have any luck at all in finding witnesses at the site of either stabbing? Or anything out of the ordinary, such as a convenient distraction at the time they must have taken place? It occurred to me that if their attention was drawn elsewhere, neither Mr Holt nor Mr Bellamy might have been as alert as they normally would have been."

Reed appeared to be thinking this over. "As you can appreciate, one of the obstacles we have faced is the gap in time between the stabbing and the time the two men died. There was no obvious disturbance. By the time it was realized anything was amiss, an attacker would have had plenty of time to disappear into a crowd, into a building, do something to change their appearance ... the list goes on."

"I do appreciate that, Inspector. So there were no witnesses that you could find?"

"The only witness, if we may call him that, was John Meredith, the passenger in Bellamy's cab when he was attacked. He says he saw nothing out of the ordinary, and perhaps he didn't, but at least we know he was looking directly at Bellamy and his cab at the crucial time. To that end, I have requested Mr Meredith to accompany us to Carfax in an attempt to recreate the scene as far as possible. He has agreed to that, and I have found a cab driver willing to play the role of William Bellamy."

"That is a good idea," Theo said. "Memory is an odd thing, and he may recall something that meant nothing to him at the time. When are you hoping to stage this recreation?"

"Tomorrow, at roughly the same hour as the original attack. Why – are you planning to hover in the background?"

Theo smiled. "Possibly. Mrs Miles and I need to collect our wedding invitations from the printer in the High, so we would have a legitimate reason for being there. May I ask who else knows about your plan?"

"Only Gregory Holt and Mrs Georgia Holt, although I haven't asked either of them to be present. I simply told them we were planning a reconstruction in the hope of finding more information. Neither objected. I don't want an audience, nor do I want to alert anyone to what we are doing, since I wish the scene to be as normal as it was that day. If you feel obliged to attend, I would ask you to keep quiet and observe."

"I promise we will. Inspector, why do you think whoever stabbed Timothy Holt didn't bother to rob him at the same time? Didn't that strike you as odd?"

The question surprised Reed, Theo noted, which proved that the neighborhood gossip had been accurate. The inspector didn't bother to ask where Theo had learned this, but simply said, "I agree it is odd, but I don't know. Perhaps he merely was in a hurry to remove himself from the scene. Or he may have been expecting pay from another source for carrying out the attack."

"And how about Mr Bellamy? Was he robbed? A cab driver might be expected to be carrying a reasonable amount of money from his fares, perhaps more than Mr Holt."

"That is true, although I don't believe robbery was the motive in either case, which disposes of Mrs Holt's theory of a random street ruffian attacking her husband. He was the target, just as Bellamy was later. Since you ask, we found the money Bellamy was carrying in a leather purse on the floor, under the driver's seat by his feet, or where his feet would have been if he hadn't fallen off."

"Interesting," Theo said. "Had he been carrying it under his coat rather than placing it by his feet, it may have deflected the knife."

"Possibly. I imagine he was carrying it whilst speaking to Mr Meredith, and then placed it under the seat before climbing onto it. We don't know exactly when he was struck."

"Before he got onto the driver's seat, at any rate. His attacker could hardly have been airborne, or even on the roof of the cab."

"You don't need to point out the obvious," Reed said, a little testily. "My theory is that they approached him and either distracted his attention for a moment, or pretended to bump into him. They stabbed him and then rapidly melted into the background before Bellamy or anyone else realized what had happened. Bellamy had enough strength to climb onto the seat and start off, but not more."

Theo nodded in agreement, since that scenario was the only one that made sense.

"That argues that there was nothing about the attacker's appearance to be at all notable. How frustrating for you, Inspector. Did Mr Bellamy have a wife in whom he may have confided any details of Mr Holt's last journey?"

"Alas, no. He was a widower."

"Or fellow drivers? The one who drove us the other day knew he had been questioned by the police."

"We have spoken to as many as we could locate. The consensus was that he was more aggrieved by the fact that he had to clean out his cab and waste his time, as he put it, speaking to the police, than any helpful details about Timothy Holt."

Sergeant Bennett loomed in the doorway, carrying an immense teapot. He nodded to Theo and silently refilled the cups.

"Thank you," Theo said. "In case you're wondering, Sergeant, I haven't come to provide the missing bit of evidence to resolve two murders. I wish I could have done."

"Pity that," Bennett said. "I don't fancy having to visit that Mrs Holt again, but I reckon we will, in case she thinks of something helpful. Sayin' her husband was some kind of saint who never did nothing wrong or upset anybody ain't exactly useful."

"Or truthful," Theo said. "Gregory Holt confirmed that his sister-in-law was fully aware of his brother's liaison with Miss Appleby, although he didn't say when she may have learned of it. We can assume that whenever that was, she wasn't pleased by it."

Bennett chuckled suddenly. "Can't really blame him, though. Mebbe you ain't seen Mrs Holt, but you've seen Miss Appleby, and most men would rather have a nice armful like her rather than a little woman with no more meat on her than a ha'penny rabbit. And a face to match."

"Sergeant," Reed said, a warning in his voice, but Theo grinned, reflecting that he considered Rose to be a perfect shape, neither too slender nor too plump, and lovely as well, with her fair hair and dark blue eyes. Then his smile faded as an idea crept into his mind.

"Is Mrs Holt rather thin and small, then?" he asked.

"Arr, and her a mother of five, too. Amazin'. We've got four and my missus just got bigger with every one, not that I mind."

Theo looked at Reed. "If dressed appropriately, could Mrs Holt pass in a crowd as a young lad?"

"Possibly," Reed said. "I see what you are suggesting. She is no more than five feet tall, and quite thin. But in order to do that, she would have to be in the right place at the right time, and there's no indication she wasn't at home when her husband was killed."

"Servants can lie or simply be unobservant, and children might not notice, if they are being looked after by a nursemaid or governess. Two sons are away at school anyway. I understand her brother lives with the family – what did he say?"

"Daniel Shepherd," Reed said, "probably wouldn't notice if his brother-in-law was stabbed and bled to death in front of him. That is a statement of fact, not a criticism."

Theo remembered Mrs Minton's assessment of Shepherd as a dreamer, somewhat out of touch with reality. It seemed the police shared that view.

"That doesn't make him a very helpful witness," he said, "but it doesn't make him a murderer, either."

"No, it doesn't."

"He'd forget who he was meant to be stabbing," Bennett said. "We talked to him more than once and he answered all right, but it was like he weren't really there or not paying attention. Said we were takin' him from his work and disruptin' his train of thought. That train already jumped the tracks, if you ask me."

Theo knew what it was like to forget time or place while in the process of creation, but Bennett added, "Not that he's half-witted or anything like that. We had a look in his room, and there's sheets of paper all over the place. Not just words on them, but lots of numbers, like drawings, almost."

"I believe they are mathematical or scientific calculations," Reed said. "He has some sort of laboratory set up in the cellar of the house and spends much of his time there."

Theo was intrigued by the idea of a secret laboratory in the cellar of an outwardly respectable residence in a quiet Oxford street. He made a mental note to include such a place in his next novel.

"What does he do there, do you know?" he asked.

"I'm afraid not. It hardly seemed to be relevant to the death of his brother-in-law. And before you ask, the servants have been told to leave his laboratory and his room alone, so they couldn't say whether he'd been there at the relevant time or not."

"You're speaking of the time of Timothy Holt's death," Theo said.

"Yes."

"What about when Mr Bellamy was killed?"

"He said he was out. When asked where, he said he couldn't remember."

"Do you believe him?"

"No."

"I wouldn't, either. So I assume you will be asking him several more times until you get an coherent answer. Tell me, Inspector, when you first spoke to Mrs Holt, the day her husband died, did you mention the name of the cab driver to her? Or to Mr Shepherd?"

"I didn't," Reed said. "Sergeant, do you know if anyone else did?"

Bennett scratched his head, thinking. "I don't know for sure. It were Bellamy who found him dead in the cab and I ain't sure which constable got there first when he started shoutin' for one. The butler came out of the house askin' what all the ruckus was, and it could be Bellamy's name got mentioned along the way."

"Someone obviously knew who he was," Reed said. "Someone who committed the first murder and was afraid Bellamy would identify them. So it doesn't necessarily have to be a member of the Holt household."

"No, it doesn't. I just wondered why it took them a fortnight before they managed to find him again and commit the second murder. I know there are quite a few cab drivers in Oxford, but if they killed Timothy Holt, they knew what Mr Bellamy, his horse and his cab all looked like. I believe the cabs have identifying numbers on them don't they? So it almost seems as if for some reason, they didn't have the opportunity to locate him."

Reed frowned at him. "I hope, after all this, you're not suggesting Miss Appleby couldn't locate him because she was in prison."

"No, I'm not, if only because she has never had a credible reason to want Timothy Holt dead. But isn't it possible that his killer didn't think at first there were any possible witnesses to his crime, and then it later occurred to him that the cab driver might be able to identify him? So after a gap of several days, he set out to find that particular cab driver to safeguard against being named. And at the time he found him and killed him, Miss Appleby was still locked up, wasn't she?"

"Yes."

"So we are back at the first murder, aren't we?"

"*We*?" Reed asked, lifting his eyebrows.

"The police, of course," Theo said, trying to sound repentant. "If I were you, however, there is one question I would want answered."

"Only one?"

"To begin with. Where was Irene Appleby when Timothy Holt was killed? She did not call into the millinery where she claimed to be going. She said she was meeting someone but refuses to say who that was. I'd want that question answered before any others."

Bennett cleared his throat. "That ain't quite the question, Mr Stone, if you don't mind me sayin' so. It's not so much *who* she was meeting' or *where* she was meeting' them, but *why* she don't want to tell us either of those things."

EIGHTEEN

"I agree, and I would assume she is trying to protect someone," Theo said. "Wouldn't you, Inspector?"

"Or trying to protect herself."

Theo thought of Rose and his mother, immediately thinking of a deeply personal reason why Irene wouldn't have wanted to say where she was going. Perhaps there wasn't even a second person involved and she had simply invented them rather than reveal her true destination.

"I don't think so, unless it was something so personal or embarrassing that she doesn't want to say. I believe it's more likely that she has a strong suspicion of who stabbed Mr Holt, but for whatever reason, doesn't want to identify them."

"Which could put her in serious danger," Reed said. "Blast the woman. I'm beginning to wish I'd left her in prison until she became more communicative."

"You would have had a long wait, I suspect," Theo said. "Inspector, I know this is not my affair to manage …"

"But you're going to meddle anyway."

"It's only a suggestion, which you are free to discard. In the event that Mrs Holt did disguise herself as a young lad – something you admit is possible – would it not be an idea to have such a lad as part of your reconstruction? And if she didn't, no harm would be done. I can offer a candidate."

"Who?"

"Jem, the bright lad who works as a bellboy at the Randolph. Remember him? Not only would he be willing to help, I'm sure, but since he is normally to be found on the corner of Beaumont Street, he may even have been a witness to the attack on Mr Holt. I doubt anyone questioned him."

Reed tapped his fingers on the table while he considered the idea. He had met Jem, who although only about twelve or thirteen years old, was both intelligent and observant. He had played a crucial role in a previous case, so Reed knew he could be trusted and could think quickly in an emergency.

"Very well. If you bring him to Carfax at about half one tomorrow afternoon, I will brief him on what he should do, and perhaps more importantly, what he should not do. If his employers at the Randolph are reluctant to let him go for an hour or so, tell them they will be compensated for the temporary loss of his services."

"Jem will be thrilled to know he is playing an active part, even if the reconstruction fails to identify the murderer." Theo got to his feet. "Thank you for the tea, and I shall see you tomorrow afternoon."

Theo left the police station, wondering if Georgia Holt had indeed managed to slip out of her house, disguised as a young man, and had followed her husband to the home of his mistress. Or conversely, she might have guessed where he was going and got there first, waiting until he appeared in Beaumont Street to hail a cab.

And then what? Theo stopped in the middle of the busy Cornmarket, causing a housewife carrying a basket of vegetables to bump into him from behind.

"I do apologize," he said, noting that his abrupt halt had caused the basket to tip half its contents into the street. "Totally my fault. Let me help you."

He bent down to collect three potatoes, two turnips and chased a small head of cabbage which had merrily rolled away. He returned them to the basket, and again had a sudden mental image of someone creating a similar disturbance just before Timothy Holt had embarked on his final journey. It wouldn't have to be runaway vegetables, but anything that would distract Holt just long enough for someone to sidle up and stab him. One strong, hard thrust with a sharp blade in the right place might have been all that was needed.

But the idea that had caused him to stop so suddenly was still in his mind. If Georgia had killed her husband, how had she arrived home so quickly that she had been there ahead of Bellamy's cab carrying her fatally wounded husband?

Even by hailing another cab, she would have been fortunate to get there first. And she had been at home, as far as he knew, when the first constable had arrived in response to Bellamy's grim discovery. How long had that taken?

Theo could see what had seemed a viable theory disappearing as a possibility. That was frustrating, and he only hoped that the reconstruction would jog someone's memory.

He gave the vegetable carrier a last warm smile and set off again, dodging black-gowned students and street peddlers until he reached the end of Cornmarket and the pedestrian and vehicular traffic thinned. Another few minutes and he was at the Randolph Hotel on the corner of Beaumont Street.

The Randolph was the grandest hotel in Oxford and Theo knew Jem was grateful to have a post there, never mind that he worked long hours carrying heavy bags for guests who might or might not give him a small tip to supplement his meagre wages. In the rare hours when he was not on duty, he was allowed to curl up and sleep on a thin mattress, after devouring just enough food to keep him going.

Despite all this, Jem was confident to the point of cockiness, and had expressed an interest in joining the constabulary when he was old enough. That alone made Theo sure he would be happy to participate in a police activity.

He waited until Jem appeared on the steps, struggling to carry a leather suitcase that was almost as big as he was. He handed it over to the waiting carriage driver and then caught sight of Theo. A grin lit up his face and he came over.

"Carry your bag, mister?"

"You know I haven't got one, Jem. I've come to ask your help, or rather I've been authorized by Inspector Reed to ask your help."

Jem's eyes widened. "Doin' what, sir?"

Theo explained briefly what the police had in mind, not mentioning the possibility of a respectable matron masquerading as a boy of Jem's age.

"So I'd be almost like a constable, then?"

"In a way. I'll have to speak to the hotel manager to get permission for you to be away from your post for a while."

"Don't know if she'll go for that."

Theo remembered that unusually, the Randolph's manager was a woman. He hoped that what Rose described as his charming manner, added to the police promise of payment, would be enough to sway her opinion.

"Let's find out. Where would she be?"

As he had hoped, the promise of cold hard cash was enough to persuade the manageress to dispense with Jem's services for an hour or so the following day. Jem himself was delighted, since Theo imagined he rarely was allowed time enough leave the hotel premises.

"Do you know, Jem, I don't believe we've ever been formally introduced," he said, as they returned to the hotel reception area.

"No, sir, don't reckon we have been, but you told her you was Theodore Stone."

"That's right. My friends call me Theo."

"Friends like that lady you was with before?"

"Yes, although she's a bit more than a friend."

Jem grinned knowingly and Theo suspected he'd seen quite a few couples at the hotel claiming to be married who had no legal documents to back that up.

"Thought she might be. She's a looker, she is. I'm Jeremy Little, and you needn't say anything; I've heard it all before."

Theo couldn't help smiling, since he was sure Jem's quick wits had put more than one would-be tormentor in their place. The name was fitting, however, Jem being no more than five feet tall and thin as a rail.

"So I'll come by here tomorrow, just after one o'clock," he said, "and we'll go to Carfax, where the inspector will explain what you need to do. It won't be difficult."

"Will it be dangerous?" Jem asked hopefully.

"I shouldn't think so. But it could be very useful."

"You can count on me, Mister."

Theo stopped at Rose's house on his way back, to tell her about the planned crime scene reconstruction and Jem's temporary recruitment into police ranks.

"He'll be thrilled," he predicted. "And it shouldn't be at all dangerous, even though he rather hopes it will be."

"He could be very helpful," Rose said. "I remember how observant he was in the Burton case. And his quick wits kept the murderer from escaping. I suppose he would have been apprehended soon enough, but Jem's actions hastened the process."

"They did indeed. Now, if you would like to attend this reconstruction with Jem and myself, we will be leaving just after one o'clock."

"You couldn't keep me away," Rose said. "I don't know how much the reconstruction will help, but one never knows. Someone's memory may be jogged by it, preferable Mr Meredith's. I can't help thinking he must have seen *something* out of the ordinary."

"One would think so, but perhaps his full attention was simply on getting a cab and traveling home."

"Perhaps," Rose said doubtfully. "Well, we shall see. I thought I would go to the millinery tomorrow morning and collect the hat I ordered, but I will be home well before midday. We can have something to eat and then collect Jem on the way."

"That sounds an excellent plan. Whilst we're in the High, we could see if Mr Nichols has printed our invitations yet."

"That's a good idea."

"So I will take my leave now," Theo said, "and go back to work on *Honesty for Sale*. Publishers must be placated to make them happy and keep the money rolling in."

"I quite understand. Will you return here for an evening meal? I'll tell Cook if you do."

"I will, if you don't mind. I think I shall need all my strength tomorrow."

Rose was awake early the next morning, her mind full of the plans for the day. The new hat should be waiting for her, so she would collect it, and then after lunch, there was the crime scene reconstruction at Carfax. That was almost exciting enough to compensate for the fact that she still felt obliged to dress in black while in public.

Cora brought her morning tea and Rose drank it gratefully before dressing and going downstairs for breakfast. She sat at the table and as she had for the last two months since their engagement, pictured Theo sitting opposite her, probably with a plate of bacon and fried eggs or some other hearty breakfast suitable for a male appetite. Cook would like that, too, since making tea, toast and the occasional boiled egg was hardly a challenge to her culinary talents.

That thought made Rose smile, and she finished her toast and a second cup of tea before putting on her hat and coat for the trip to the millinery. She had a feeling Cora would have liked to be asked to accompany her, but for some reason, Rose felt she should go alone.

She stepped out into a cold, crisp morning, enjoying the winter sunshine as she walked toward Little Clarendon Street. There weren't many people out this early in the day, and Rose amused herself by observing the ones she passed and pretending to describe them to someone official, such as Inspector Reed.

There was a large woman dressed in something that Rose thought resembled drawing room curtains, sailing along the pavement like a stately galleon. Two younger women were chatting and giggling together as they looked in shop windows, probably debating whether to buy a new hat or gloves. They looked enough alike that Rose supposed they were sisters, both with fair hair pinned up under fashionable bonnets.

Two smartly dressed men passed them going the opposite direction, deeply engrossed in conversation.

Then she froze. Fifty yards or so ahead of her was a woman dressed in head to toe black, but the glowing auburn hair visible under the edge of the hat was unmistakeable. Irene Appleby was walking briskly along, ignoring the enticing shop displays and obviously on her way to a specific destination.

Rose decided the new hat could wait a little longer. She picked up her pace and followed Irene as she reached the next street and paused. Irene turned to look down the street, glanced back over her shoulder, and saw Rose.

There was nothing for it. Rose had to keep walking until she was in earshot, because Irene made no effort to move on.

"Good morning, Miss Appleby," she said, trying for a calm, cheerful tone. "How pleasant to see you again."

"Good morning, Mrs Miles. May I ask – are you following me?"

"Not at all," Rose said. "I am on my way to the millinery in Little Clarendon Street to collect a hat I have ordered."

Since that was true, she felt little guilt in saying it.

"May I accompany you?" Irene sounded skeptical, not that Rose blamed her.

"By all means. I would be glad of your company. The streets are not always safe, are they?"

She assumed Irene had asked to accompany her to discover whether she was telling the truth about the hat, and was amused when she turned to walk beside Rose. They reached the millinery without further conversation, and at the door, Rose said, "I hope I am not keeping you from some other appointment."

"No. I was simply out for a walk."

"I see."

"You don't believe me."

"Let's say I am somewhat skeptical."

"That is your privilege."

Rose couldn't argue with that. "Would you care to come inside whilst I collect my order?"

"Certainly."

The milliner obviously remembered Rose, and cast a glance at Irene which made Rose wonder if she had been believed when she had said she was a widow about to marry for a second time. It would be embarrassing to be thought to be some wealthy man's mistress, simply because she was in the company of someone who had been just that. She could only hope the milliner knew nothing of Irene's domestic arrangement.

But the woman said nothing beyond a pleasant greeting and went to fetch Rose's new hat. It was just as pretty as she remembered, the soft gray a sober but flattering color. Rose handed over the payment and the hat was put into a box for carrying.

"It's a very attractive hat," Irene said when they were outside again. "I can see why you chose it."

"Yes, I think it is. I plan to wear it at my wedding." Since Irene seemed marginally more friendly now, she decided to press on. "One does get so very tired of being dressed in black, day after day. It is not that one wishes to be disrespectful, but after a while, it becomes extremely depressing. I find myself longing for a bit of bright color, as I am sure you will, too."

Irene looked at Rose's black coat, hat and gloves and then down at her own black coat.

"We must look like a pair of crows," she said, a smile flickering across her face. "You are quite right to suggest I have no obligation to wear mourning, perhaps not even any right to, but I feel that I should, at least for a while."

"Of course. You were fond of Mr Holt."

"Very fond indeed. I apologize for doubting your purpose, Mrs Miles. It's only that since Timothy died, and his killer not yet apprehended, I find myself very nervous about anything out of the ordinary. When I saw you walking behind me, I couldn't help thinking it was for some sinister purpose."

"I quite understand. I think in your position, I should feel the same."

"I was only going to a nearby shop, but I keep thinking that they might see me as a threat to their safety and …" She made a helpless gesture with her gloved hand.

"Why?" Rose asked. "If there is anything that might help the police, you really must tell them. That would help ensure your own safety as well."

Irene didn't answer. Rose resisted the impulse to take her by the shoulders and shake her.

"Please forgive the familiarity, but Irene, I am sure you know something that you are holding back. Why won't you say?"

Irene bit her lower lip but still said nothing.

"The day Mr Holt died, you said you were going to the millinery. You weren't. You were going to meet with someone. Can you tell me who that was?"

Irene's green eyes met Rose's. "I met with no one."

"Then why say you did?"

"I never said I 'met' with anyone. I said, quite honestly, that I 'went to meet' with someone. They requested the meeting. But when I arrived at the appointed place, no one was there. I waited for a while, then went back home. It wasn't until I heard of Timothy's death that I realized I had been tricked, put into a position where I couldn't prove I hadn't killed him."

Rose thought about that and was forced to agree. Someone had neatly maneuvered Irene into a corner where she had no way of proving where she had been at the crucial time. No witnesses, no one to confirm her statement. Her servants would say, truthfully, that she hadn't been at home. It was no wonder the police had been skeptical, even an inspector as experienced and intelligent as Matthew Reed. And while Irene was waiting for someone who had no intention of meeting her, Timothy Holt had been murdered.

There was only one question to ask, and she asked it.

"Irene, who was it who asked you to meet with them? Please tell me."

NINETEEN

It was clear that Irene did not want to answer Rose's question, and equally clear that she longed to confide in someone. The strain of keeping the secret was beginning to tell. Rose did her best to look honest, sympathetic and helpful.

Finally, Irene said, "If I tell you, I assume you will go straight to the police."

"Not necessarily. There must be a reason why you have not told them before, not even to keep yourself from being imprisoned."

"A good reason, and it has nothing to do with protecting myself. I have spent most of my life looking after my own interests and I shall continue to do so."

"I believe you. Who asked you to meet with them?"

"Georgia Holt."

Now that she had the answer they had been seeking, Rose was not quite sure what to make of it. Did that mean Georgia Holt had intended to have Irene blamed for the murder of her husband? Or was Georgia not even involved in either the message or the murder?

"Are you certain the message was from her?" she asked. "After all, it would be fairly simple for anyone who knew about your arrangement with Mr Holt to send a message in her name, knowing you would be tempted to respond."

"But no one knew …" Irene stopped, perhaps because of the look on Rose's face.

"I'm afraid," Rose said gently, "your relationship was far more widely known than you might have imagined. Women with little to do all day enjoy sharing gossip, whether or not based on facts. In your case, of course, the rumors were true."

"I can see I have been rather naïve," Irene said, after a moment of silence. "I don't have women friends, so I underestimated the spread of gossip, or how enjoyable that might be for the participants. Thank you for enlightening me, Mrs Miles."

Rose ignored the slight tinge of sarcasm. "I wish I hadn't had to. But you didn't answer my question. Are you positive Mrs Holt sent the message?"

Irene made a motion with her hand, as if brushing cobwebs from her face. "Now that you ask, no, I suppose not. I simply assumed she had sent it. It seemed believable that she would do such a thing."

"If you don't mind telling me, what did it say?"

"It said my relationship with Timothy would soon be coming to an end. Whoever sent it knew he was coming to see me that day because they said that after he left, they would meet me to discuss my future."

"That sounds rather ominous. So you went to meet with them."

"Yes, and no one was there. In hindsight, I suppose I was foolish. But of course, they were quite right in that our relationship did indeed come to an end."

"And the message was signed by Mrs Holt?"

"Yes."

"Written by hand?"

"Yes, and delivered by a messenger. Having never seen her writing, I can't say it was hers."

"So it may not have been." Rose felt a wave of sympathy for Irene, whose usual self-confidence had visibly lessened. "It does seem clear that whoever sent the message – Mrs Holt or someone else – knew where you lived, and intended that you should be unable to say where you were at the time Mr Holt was killed. And that argues that they knew he was about to die."

"Yes, I now realize that. At the time, I merely thought they were threatening to make our arrangement public knowledge, or something else which would make it impossible to continue. After all, Timothy had said he might not be able to see me for a while. But then when he died …" Her voice quavered.

"You realized it may have meant something far more sinister. But why keep the knowledge to yourself?"

Irene looked at her incredulously, her green eyes wide and troubled.

"Need you ask? Because I was convinced his wife had killed him, or had arranged for someone else to do so. However much I wanted revenge for his death, I couldn't be responsible for leaving five children as orphans. If she had been convicted and hanged for his murder, what would have happened to them? The youngest one is only five years old. I was an orphan – under different circumstances, I admit – but I couldn't do that to them. I simply couldn't."

"Your kindness does you credit," Rose said, meaning it sincerely, "but it may mean they have been left with a mother who has murdered their father. It is debateable which would be worse. However, she may not have been involved at all, you know, if someone else sent that message in her name."

"I hope that is the case."

"Did you keep the message?"

"No. Once I had noted the time and place of the meeting, I threw it into the fire."

"That's a pity," Rose said. "I can see why you did that, but in hindsight, it would have been useful to have kept it. But I do think the police must be told. Will you do that, or would you rather I did?"

"I don't think I could face them just yet. But I can't ask you to do something I am too cowardly to do for myself."

Rose thought quickly. "There may be a third way. This afternoon, the police are attempting to stage a reconstruction of the scene where the cab driver, William Bellamy, was killed. They know you could not have committed that crime. If the person who killed both Mr Holt and Mr Bellamy can be identified, then you would never have to tell anyone about the message."

"Are you suggesting I watch this reconstruction?"

Rose hadn't actually meant to suggest that, but she didn't think there would be any reason why Irene shouldn't be there.

"If you wish, although I don't think you should advertise your presence. Simply pretend to be a passer-by. It will be between half one and two at Carfax."

"Thank you, Mrs Miles," Irene said. "I will be there."

"I may have been foolish in suggesting she could come to the reconstruction," Rose said to Theo some time later. "But she has a justified interest in finding Mr Holt's killer, if not Mr Bellamy's. If she decides to attend, I do hope Mrs Holt is not also present. Assuming she knows anything of Irene's appearance and can identify her, that could be extremely awkward."

"It could indeed. Inspector Reed didn't know if she would attend, although she is aware of it. Since she is in the first stages of mourning, one would think not."

I don't know," Rose said doubtfully. "She might think it her duty to be there, and as I know, any excuse to escape the confines of one's house is welcome in those early stages."

"So we will be watching for a small, thin woman swathed in black mourning clothes, taking an intense interest in the proceedings whilst pretending not to do so."

"Something like that, yes. Theo, I think Miss Appleby is walking on a thin line, emotionally speaking. She desperately wants Mr Holt's killer to be found, and she believes it was his wife, but she would prefer it to be someone else, for the children's sake."

"There's nothing we can do about that, my dear," Theo said. "I appreciate her concern, but if Georgia Holt stabbed her husband and an innocent cab driver to death, she can't be allowed to escape justice. Who knows who else she might consider a threat? And if it is someone else, then Miss Appleby can at least know her intentions were sound."

"You're right, of course." Rose sighed. "Well, we can only hope this case is brought to some sort of satisfactory conclusion this afternoon, no matter who is hurt in the process."

They both tried to keep that thought in mind as they ate their lunch. Rose found she didn't have much appetite, but it would take more than an attempt to corner a double murderer to put a dent in Theo's appreciation of Cook's creations.

She had provided them with a casserole, chunks of chicken and vegetables in a rich gravy and topped with fluffy dumplings. Theo devoured his share, pausing only to comment that Cook's casserole was to Mrs Rice's stew as a thoroughbred racehorse was to a broken down cart nag.

"I shouldn't criticize, as she does the best she can with her limited budget, but this is so much tastier."

"I'm glad you like it." Rose regarded her half-eaten portion with some dismay. "It's nothing to do with Cook's talents, but I find I am not really very hungry."

Theo reached over and touched her hand. "I know you're worried that Miss Appleby may be correct and if she is, then the Holt children will be facing a very difficult time. But perhaps their uncle will be able to step in."

"Which uncle? If your mother and Mrs Minton are correct, I can't see Mr Shepherd being of much assistance."

"No, I was thinking more of Gregory Holt. It would be a brave person who angered him by tormenting his nieces and nephews."

"True."

There was fresh fruit to follow the main course, and then it was time to go. Rose put her black coat and hat on again and took Theo's arm, feeling the need for physical as well as emotional support. They walked down St Giles toward the Randolph Hotel and Rose said, "I wonder if Jem has any clothing other than his bellboy's uniform. He would be rather recognizable in that, wouldn't he?"

"I never thought of that," Theo said. "We'll see."

In the event, they needn't have worried. Jem was wearing the striped trousers and short jacket he wore on duty, but he had covered most of his body with a long black coat which had clearly been intended for someone larger. It hung down to his ankles, and in lieu of gloves he had simply pulled the over-long sleeves to cover his hands and jammed them into the pockets.

"Good afternoon, Jem," Theo said. "You remember Mrs Miles, I think."

"Sure do. Afternoon, ma'am."

"Good afternoon," Rose said. "That coat looks very warm, Jem. I'm glad you have it."

"Piece of luck, that were," Jem confided. "Some old cove – sorry, some gennulman – left it in his room. Never came back for it, so I just … borrowed it."

"I see."

Jem strolled along beside Theo as they walked the length of Cornmarket and approached Carfax. As usual, it was busy, pedestrians, vehicles and vendors all vying for space in the crossroads. Jem's eyes were wide with wonder, taking it all in, and Theo suspected he had never been this far into the center of Oxford before.

On the corner diagonally from the clock tower, Inspector Reed was waiting, Sergeant Bennett standing a discreet distance away and keeping an eye on the activity. A hansom cab pulled up and a well-dressed, middle-aged man disembarked, looked around and then walked over to Reed.

"That must be Mr Meredith," Theo said quietly. "When he's finished his conversation with the inspector, we can take Jem to be given his instructions."

The two seemed to be discussing something in depth, and Jem shifted restlessly from one foot to the other. Finally, Meredith walked across to stand under the clock tower and Reed beckoned to Theo.

"May I introduce Master Jeremy Little?" Theo said, as they came up to the inspector. "Known as Jem. I can vouch for his honesty and integrity, and you are already acquainted with his intelligence and powers of observation. Jem, this gentleman is Inspector Reed. He'll tell you what you are to do."

"Yes, sir."

Jem stood to attention, and Theo added, "Mrs Miles has found the answer you were seeking earlier, Inspector. At about the same time Timothy Holt was killed, Miss Appleby went to an appointment that she thought was with Mrs Holt. No one was there to meet with her, so we can assume it was an attempt to leave her without an alibi."

"I see," Reed said thoughtfully. "Thank Mrs Miles for that piece of information, will you?"

"I will."

Theo went back to Rose's side. "Should we go into the printer's shop?" she asked. "We don't want to be obviously waiting for something to happen."

"I suppose we could do. At least hover in the doorway, where we'll have a good view."

It was tempting, but curiosity kept them both rooted to the spot. Reed was explaining something to Jem, who was nodding furiously. As Theo and Rose watched, the boy took up a position on the far side of Carfax, half hidden behind a vendor selling roasted chestnuts. Rose suddenly clutched Theo's arm.

"Look, over there."

As she had been earlier, Irene Appleby was dressed in black, but her auburn hair was hard to completely conceal, and was visible between her hat and the collar of her coat. She was simply walking along, pausing to look in shop windows, giving a good imitation of a casual passer-by.

Theo took out his pocket watch. "Nearly two o'clock," he said. "That was about when Mr Bellamy must have been attacked. So I assume the curtain is about to go up."

A hansom cab rolled along Queen Street and crossed Carfax. John Meredith, who had been consulting his watch, put it into his pocket and hurried after the cab, which had come to a halt on the far side of the crossroads, at the top of the High Street. The driver climbed down and began to adjust the horse's bridle.

As he did, Theo noticed Sergeant Bennett drifting along the road and followed his progress. The sergeant stopped just behind two people who were avidly watching the reconstruction, a man in his forties and a short, thin woman dressed all in black.

By mutual, unspoken consent, Theo and Rose moved into earshot, standing a few feet behind the trio.

Meredith came up to the driver and appeared to ask a question. The driver turned away, gesturing down the High

Street with one arm raised. Suddenly, a small figure in a long black coat darted in between the people and vehicles on the street. He ran straight toward the driver, diving under his raised arm and nearly knocking him off his feet. The driver swore, there was a brief wrestling match and then Jem was slung to one side, stumbling before regaining his balance.

Meredith turned to look across at Reed, who nodded to Bennett.

"And that's how it could be done," Theo murmured to Rose. "A shorter person, barging into him at chest height."

"Yes, but proving *how* it could be done doesn't prove *who* did it," Rose objected. "It's a step forward, to be sure, but …"

They both started in surprise as the man standing by Bennett began to shout.

"There she is. Arrest her, Sergeant!"

Irene Appleby, who had been walking along slowly, stopped and turned. Theo and Rose moved closer.

"Are you referring to me, sir?"

"Of course I am. Jade, dolly mop, slut …"

"Be quiet, Daniel." Georgia Holt's voice was tense. "She isn't worth the trouble."

"I won't be quiet. I won't." Daniel Shepherd sounded more like a stubborn child than an adult, and it was obvious his sister was desperately trying to silence him.

"Do you have something constructive to contribute, Mr Shepherd?" Reed asked. "You know why we staged this situation; to try and determine how Mr Bellamy could have been attacked. And a fortnight ago, how the same technique could have been used to kill your brother-in-law. A young lad, for example, armed with a sharp blade, or even one merely creating a distraction."

"Yes, that must have been what happened," Georgia Holt said quickly. "Some opportunistic thief, attempting to rob my husband and later, this unfortunate cab driver."

Daniel Shepherd was staring at his sister, his expression one of disbelief. Then he turned to Reed.

"You have it all wrong."

"Do we?" Reed asked calmly.

"That isn't how it happened at all. It wasn't some wretched street urchin who killed either of them!"

"Daniel!" Mrs Holt was furious, grabbing his arm. "Don't say any more."

But there was no stopping Shepherd, who had lost any vestige of propriety or it seemed, self-preservation.

"I killed both of them, and I don't regret it for a minute!"

He yanked his arm away from her and started to turn away, only to find himself facing Irene, who hadn't moved.

"Why?" she asked. "What harm did either of them do to you?"

"It was you," Shepherd said, almost spitting the words. "Timothy refused to give me a penny for my research, but he was going to pay a fortune for you to start a school for street brats. He thought that was a good idea, but he wouldn't listen to me, when my research could have saved mankind. I pleaded with him and he laughed in my face. Said your school was a far more sensible idea. Sensible? A school for brats, run by a slut? So he deserved to die, and it's your fault he did."

During this tirade, Irene's face had gone so pale that she appeared about to faint. Georgia Holt's complexion was nearly as bleached, as she stared at her brother, leaving Theo to wonder if it was because she had never suspected him, or because she had somehow collaborated with him in the two murders.

"Daniel Shepherd," Reed said, "I am arresting you in the name of …"

He got no further. Shepherd whirled around, pushed his way past Bennett and raced across the street to where the cab driver, having finished his part in the reconstruction, was chatting to John Meredith on the pavement. As a result, both of them were caught by surprise when Shepherd jumped onto the driver's seat and slapped the reins on the horse's back.

"Oi, get off there!" the driver shouted. He grabbed for the harness, but the obedient horse had started off and the cab was rolling down the High Street, Shepherd using the whip to get the horse to pick up his pace.

The police were also caught by surprise, Reed gesturing to Bennett to stay with Mrs Holt while he blew his whistle to summon more constables. Theo and Rose watched in astonishment as Shepherd tried to force his way down the street.

"He can't be trying to get away, can he?" Rose said. "He must know he won't get far and may injure someone before he's stopped."

Pedestrians were scattered like ninepins as the cab moved along, but it was forced to stop for a minute as a carriage blocked its path. Theo looked at Reed and then at Rose.

"I know it's mad, but I'm going to try," he said, and before either of them could object, he began to run after the cab. He reached it just as it started to move again, swinging himself onto the side board, clinging to the door and hoping Shepherd wouldn't think to use the whip to knock him off.

"What on earth does he think he's doing?" Reed demanded of Rose. "He needs to leave this to the police. If Shepherd has a knife with him …"

"I know," Rose whispered.

TWENTY

On the cab, Theo was trying to work his way up to the driver's seat. Shepherd had been so intent on his getaway that he hadn't noticed at first that he had an unwanted passenger, but now he swung an arm out and tried to knock Theo off.

Theo dodged the blow and clung to the door. The vibration of the cab on the street stones threatened to shake him loose as the cab picked up speed again, and he wondered how long he could hang on. He managed to take off one glove and then the other to get a better grip, stuffing them in his coat pocket, and took stock of the situation.

The High Street was a very long street, and there was no indication that Shepherd intended to stop along it at any point. When he reached the Plain, he would have a choice of three roads, all of which would eventually lead out of Oxford and into the countryside.

It would be harder for the police to locate him there and also easier for him to dispose of Theo without potential witnesses. So Theo knew that if he had any chance of stopping the cab and Shepherd being apprehended, it would have to be done before they reached the end of the High Street.

He edged forward and lifted one leg to get a foot onto the floor under the driver's seat. Shepherd flailed at him with the whip, catching his bare hand and leaving a red welt across it.

The pain infuriated Theo and he managed to push himself up far enough to lunge full length at Shepherd, causing him to slide halfway across the polished wooden seat and the cab to rock violently.

The motion made Theo fall backwards, grasping the seat. He scrambled upright and gave Shepherd another shove. But Shepherd was more prepared this time and grabbed the side bar to keep from falling off. The cab careened down the street, swaying from side to side, the frightened horse almost galloping now.

"You're a fool, Shepherd," Theo shouted. "You know you'll never get away."

"I don't know who you are," Shepherd snarled, "but you won't stop me. No one will."

He rose to his feet, lifting one hand from the reins and turning to strike another blow at Theo. But with his head turned and his attention on his target, he failed to see the cart loaded with large wooden beer barrels that had pulled out of a side street and was blocking the way just ahead of him.

Theo did see it – noting in a corner of his mind that the cart came from his family's brewery – and anticipating the outcome, leaped off the cab just in time. He hit the ground with a thud that knocked the wind from him and sat up, gasping for breath.

Shepherd jerked his head back and yanked on the reins, but failed to stop as the cab swerved sideways and then crashed into the loaded cart. Shepherd was thrown off the seat and went headfirst into the barrels before slithering down the side of the vehicle and landing heavily on the street. The cab shuddered to a halt, one wheel skewed sideways and half the side smashed in where it had hit the heavy wooden cart.

The horse, amazingly, was quivering with fear but unharmed, and Theo, getting painfully to his feet, went over and tried to calm him.

"What in blazes was that fool … hang on, it's Mr Theodore, isn't it?" The beer delivery driver squinted down at Theo from his perch on the front of the cart. "What're you doin' here, sir? Who's he?"

He jerked a thumb at Shepherd, who was now groaning and trying to sit up. His head was bloody, his clothing was torn, and one arm hung at an unnatural angle.

"Him? He's just a double murderer I was trying to keep from escaping," Theo said. It was hard to sound nonchalant when his hand still stung and he felt bruised from head to toe. "He's injured, as you can see, but I'd still feel better if he were tied up. You wouldn't happen to have any rope in that cart, would you?"

There was no rope handy, but with a burly delivery driver holding him down, Shepherd wasn't going to move far. Reed came running down the High Street, accompanied by two constables. Jem, determined not to miss any of the excitement, wasn't far behind them, followed at a more sedate pace by Rose, Irene, John Meredith and the hansom cab driver, who surveyed the wreckage of his vehicle with disgust.

"You'll pay for this," he told Shepherd, getting only a groan in response.

"Oh, he'll pay for more than that," Theo assured him.

The constables yanked Shepherd to his feet, bringing a cry of pain as his broken arm was wrenched.

Reed faced him and completed the sentence he had begun at the top of the street, informing Shepherd that he was being arrested in the name of Her Majesty the Queen in connection with the deaths of Timothy Holt and William Bellamy.

"I don't care what happens to me," Shepherd said defiantly, as handcuffs were fastened on his wrists. "But if you hang me, you will be depriving mankind of the secret of eternal life."

Theo and Reed exchanged glances. Theo lifted his eyebrows and Reed said, "What a shame. Take him away."

The constables marched a limping Shepherd up the street toward the police station, reminding Theo of the penultimate scene in *Honesty for Sale*. He rather regretted not having thought of a chase involving a commandeered cab, and made a mental note to include that in a future novel. In the meantime …

"Theo, are you injured?" Rose asked, looking him over worriedly.

"Only bruises and a sore hand, and my coat and trousers will need to be mended. The important thing is that the man who killed two innocent people has been apprehended."

"Yes, of course. You were very brave."

"Others might consider my actions foolish, I'm afraid."

"I wouldn't exactly describe it as foolish, although I admit I didn't expect this outcome to the reconstruction," Reed said. He cleared his throat and added, "I suppose I owe you some thanks, Mr Stone, for risking your life to try and stop Shepherd from escaping."

Theo tried to look humble and imagined he was failing completely. "I expect the police would have caught up with him at some point," he said. "Besides, it was my family's brewery cart that actually stopped him."

He thought he heard a muffled laugh from Rose and smiled at her.

"Indeed," Reed said. "I have told Sergeant Bennett to keep Mrs Holt in custody, and I will be questioning her at length later today to see how deeply involved she was in the entire matter."

"I expect she gave her brother the idea," Rose said. "Or at least she found out that her husband was intending to help fund Miss Appleby's school, and told him about that. Mr

Shepherd seems to have already held a negative opinion regarding their relationship, but the thought that money was going toward that worthy cause rather than his so-called research must have tipped him over the edge, mentally speaking."

"I believe you are correct, Mrs Miles," Reed said. "Since you and Mr Stone were instrumental in bringing the case to a conclusion, I shall call on you later and share what additional information I have learned."

"Thank you," Rose said. "We would appreciate that."

"You should have let me come with you, mister," Jem said. "I can run real fast and I'm ever so strong."

"Should the occasion ever arise again, I promise I'll call on you," Theo said. "You still played a vital role, Jem, so content yourself with that."

Irene had been watching him with interest. Now she said, "Can you read and write, Jem?"

"Nah. I know numbers, that's all, so I can tell what room cases are goin' to. No need to know more'n that."

"You'd be surprised," Irene said. "A clever lad like you needs all the tools he can acquire to get on in the world."

"I already got a post, ma'am, a good one."

"And you could get an even better one in future."

"You reckon?" Jem looked thoughtful.

"I do indeed."

"Miss Appleby," Rose said, "I believe you may have just recruited your first pupil."

It was some hours later that Reed fulfilled his promise to come by and share the additional information he had acquired. He accepted Rose's offer of a chair by the fire and Theo's offer of a glass of brandy.

"I not only owe you some thanks for your actions today, Mr Stone, but an apology as well," he said.

"For what, Inspector?"

"For dismissing your mention of Miss Appleby's proposed school as unimportant. At the time, I didn't see any connection between that and Timothy Holt's death. But further conversation with both Shepherd and Mrs Holt revealed that there was indeed a connection, and it led almost directly to Mr Holt's murder."

"Yes, we got an indication of that before he tried to bolt, didn't we? Shepherd said something about his research discovering the secret of eternal life. Some sort of elixir or potion, I suppose. Did he really believe that?"

"Oh, yes," Reed said. "He was absolutely convinced that he would eventually discover such a formula. Hence the secret experiments in the cellar of his brother-in-law's house, with the servants forbidden to enter. Servants are often illiterate and he felt they should be kept that way. After all, one wouldn't want them stumbling onto the results of his experiments, stealing them and profiting by it."

"Oh, my goodness," Rose said. "I suppose that explains the why he reacted so violently upon learning that Mr Holt was helping his mistress to fund such a school, at the same time that his own experiments had been sneered at. He firmly believed the lower classes should be kept in ignorance, especially those who might threaten his possible success. How absurd."

"I received the impression that he had always been a bit … unstable," Reed said. "But until recently, he had been harmless enough."

Theo thought of his mother and Mrs Minton describing Shepherd as a colorless, nondescript personality, somewhat detatched from reality. They had been only partially correct. Left to himself and provided with unlimited funds, he was unlikely to have ever harmed anyone.

"A dreamer," he said. "But a potentially dangerous one."

"Indeed. His sister had indulged him, giving him money from the household budget, which explains why she is now finding herself not only widowed, but rather short of funds. She will get little sympathy from Gregory Holt, who considered Shepherd an idiot and Mrs Holt a fool for funding him."

Rose said quietly, "So Miss Appleby's attempt to protect the Holt children will likely have been in vain. That's why she refused to tell you where she had gone or who she was meeting, you know. She thought Mrs Holt had killed her husband, and her conviction for the crime would leave them as orphans. Having been one herself, she didn't want that for them, especially with the notoriety that would come if their mother had been hanged for murdering their father. Did Daniel Shepherd send her that message – the one purporting to be from Mrs Holt?"

"Yes, he did." Reed smiled ruefully. "Although remarkably stupid in some ways, he was reasonably clever in others. Once he had decided to kill his brother-in-law in revenge for not funding him, he thought it would be ideal if Miss Appleby could be blamed for it. He did, after all, consider she was responsible for Timothy Holt's failure to back his efforts. So he sent her a message in a credible imitation of his sister's writing, calculating that Miss Appleby would respond. As she did."

"Did Mrs Holt have any idea of what he had done?"

"I simply don't know," Reed said. "Since he confessed to both murders, she knows nothing can save him, and now she is obviously trying to distance herself from him. Personally, I suspect she knew what he had planned, and perhaps she felt her husband deserved to die for his infidelity, but I doubt I would ever be able to prove it. Even if I could, what would the charge be? She didn't wield the knife in either attack.

"Nor did she provide the distraction, as you suggested she may have done. It was a viable theory, but Shepherd was positively boasting about the way he sidled up to his brother-in-law in Beaumont Street, dressed in workmen's clothing so he wouldn't be recognized, and drove a sharp knife into his ribs before melting back into the stream of passers-by."

"I wonder what he would have done if the attack hadn't been fatal," Theo said. "Tried again another time, perhaps? He couldn't keep sending messages to Miss Appleby, hoping to have her blamed."

"Hardly."

"Did he explain why he also felt Mr Bellamy had to die? After all, had Shepherd left him alone, you might have gone on suspecting Miss Appleby could be responsible. I don't imagine he thought of that."

"No, I don't imagine he did. He had carried out one successful murder, but it was preying on his mind that someone might have recognized him, and the most likely person was the cab driver, whom he thought had looked directly at him just before the attack. It took him a fortnight to track down Bellamy, and he told me he deeply resented having to take the time away from his research."

"Poor Mr Bellamy," Rose said. "From what you said, Inspector, he didn't notice anything out of the ordinary, and probably wouldn't have been able to positively identify Mr Holt's attacker."

"No," Reed said. "The only purpose his death served will be to make Shepherd's conviction more secure."

"And it prevented Miss Appleby from being falsely accused."

Reed appeared rather reluctant to admit Irene's innocence, but he took another sip of brandy and said, "Yes, that as well."

After Reed had gone, Theo said, "I wonder if anyone will ever discover the secret of eternal life."

"Probably not," Rose said. "Human beings weren't meant to live forever, and the world would become rather crowded after a few centuries, wouldn't it?"

"Must you always be so practical?" Theo smiled at her. "I wouldn't mind living forever, if you were with me."

Rose leaned against his shoulder. "I will be with you as long as possible," she said. "Will that be long enough?"

"I expect so."

Suddenly she sat upright. "Theo, in all the excitement, we never collected our wedding invitations from Mr Nichols. We must do that soon, perhaps tomorrow."

"Very well, under one condition."

"And what is that?"

"That we don't ride in a hansom cab when we go to collect them. After the events of today, I don't think I will ever feel safe in one again."

Thank you for reading **Oxford Jade**. If you enjoyed it, please tell your friends and leave a review!

This is the fifth book in the **Milestone Agency Victorian Mysteries** series. Other books in the series are:

Oxford Blue (1)
Oxford Brass (2)
Oxford Ivory (3)
Oxford Crimson (4)

Other books by Cynthia E. Hurst, available as e-books on all major e-book platforms and in paperback:

In 1860s Oxfordshire, a Jewish clock repairer and a thief-turned-housemaid are an unlikely but effective detective duo in the **Silver and Simm Victorian Mysteries** novels:

Tools of the Trade (1)
Forged in the Fire (2)
Writing on the Wall (3)
Stitched up in Style (4)
Ghost on the Green (5)
Pound to a Penny (6)
Bolt from the Blue (7)
Spirit of the Season (8)
Nothing but her Name (9)
Sins of the Sisters (10)
Letter of the Law (11)

Because of the Bees (12)
There for the Taking (13)
Diamond in the Dust (14)
Proof of the Pudding (15)
Grains in the Glass (16)
Out of the Ordinary (17)
Ends of the Earth (18)
Cream of the Crop (19)
Sarah's Story (Silver and Simm Victorian Mysteries companion book)

Alexandra Barton finds mystery, adventure and a touch of romance as she visits various bits of English history in the *Time Traveller Trilogy:*

Spanish Sails (Book 1)
Otherwise Engaged (Book 2)
Heard on High (Book 3)

The **R&P Labs Mysteries** feature five Seattle scientists with a talent for solving mysteries matched only by their ability to stumble over them in the first place. Follow Rob, Phil, Ellis, Virginia and Mitch in their adventures:

Mossfire (R&P Labs Mysteries 1)
Sweetwater (R&P Labs Mysteries 2)
Shellshock (R&P Labs Mysteries 3)
Angelwood (R&P Labs Mysteries 4)
Boneflower (R&P Labs Mysteries 5)
Childproof (R&P Labs Mysteries 6)

Dreamwheel (R&P Labs Mysteries 7)
Icefox (R&P Labs Mysteries 8)
Shotglass (R&P Labs Mysteries 9)
Pushover (R&P Labs Mysteries 10)
Bedrock (R&P Labs Mysteries 11)
Uprooted (R&P Labs Mysteries 12)
Four by Five (R&P Labs Mysteries Short Stories)

Meet Zukie Merlino, a totally tactless, seriously snoopy widow with a knack for getting herself involved in mysteries. Zukie and her long-suffering cousin and housemate Lou are featured in these books:

Zukie's Burglar (Zukie Merlino Mysteries 1)
Zukie's Witness (Zukie Merlino Mysteries 2)
Zukie's Suspect (Zukie Merlino Mysteries 3)
Zukie's Detective (Zukie Merlino Mysteries 4)
Zukie's Alibi (Zukie Merlino Mysteries 5)
Zukie's Evidence (Zukie Merlino Mysteries 6)
Zukie's Promise (Zukie Merlino Mysteries 7)
Zukie's Trail (Zukie Merlino Mysteries 8)
Zukie's Ghost (Zukie Merlino Mysteries 9)
Zukie's Thief (Zukie Merlino Mysteries 10)
Zukie's Holidays (Zukie Merlino Mysteries short stories)

Printed in Great Britain
by Amazon

23458874R00119